In Search of Pretty Young Black Men

ALSO BY STANLEY BENNETT CLAY

Diva: A Novel

In Search of
Pretty Young Black Men

STANLEY BENNETT CLAY

ATRIA BOOKS   New York   London   Toronto   Sydney

ATRIA BOOKS
1230 Avenue of the Americas
New York, NY 10020

ISBN: 0-7434-9715-5

First Atria Books hardcover edition January 2005

10 9 8 7 6 5 4 3 2 1

ATRIA BOOKS is a trademark of Simon & Schuster, Inc.

Manufactured in the United States of America

For information regarding special discounts for bulk purchases,
please contact Simon & Schuster Special Sales at 1-800-456-6798 or
business@simonandschuster.com

for Reny

In Search of Pretty Young Black Men

Los Angeles is wonderful. Nowhere in the United States is the Negro so well and beautifully housed, nor the average efficiency and intelligence in the colored population so high. . . . Out here in this matchless Southern California there would seem to be no limit to your opportunities, your possibilities.

—W. E. B. Du Bois, 1913

Prologue

July 2, 1985, was a typical day in Los Angeles. The sun was bright, the air was dry, and seasonal fires routinely scourged wilderness reserves and affluent hilltop enclaves all throughout the county. On this day in Baldwin Hills, fifty-three well-appointed homes and three well-placed citizens were consumed by flames, aided and abetted by Santa Ana winds. The tragic event played out nonstop on special afternoon news reports—or misreports—on every local station. Journalists reported from helicopters the flight of several black domestic workers to the streets from their employers' torched Baldwin Hills dwellings. No one stopped to notice that the white home-owners, the so-called employers, were nowhere to be found. For what the reporters of 1985 Los Angeles did not know, and would for many seasons be embarrassed by, was that the fleeing black domestics were not the domestics at all. They were not the chauffeurs, gardeners, housekeepers, and nannies. They were indeed the owners of the manors sent up in flames.

In the early 1980s Baldwin Hills was L.A.'s best-kept

secret; a hilltop community of black wealth. Up until that tragic day little was known about Baldwin Hills. Baldwin Hills was the quiet and well-behaved baby sister of such high-profile communities as Beverly Hills, Hollywood Hills, Brentwood, Westwood, Hancock Park, and Malibu.

Baldwin Hills was where muffled black pride, discreet black money, and relentless black reserve went hand in hand in hand. It's where sun-colored Creoles, blue-black Geechese, accentless Jamaicans of means, and Harvard-educated descendants of enterprising sharecroppers lorded over siesta-style mansionettes kept beautiful and clean by those next in line.

In Baldwin Hills caramel daughters stretched out by calm swimming pools and contemplated last year's affair, the usual pilgrimage to the islands, and Wanda Coleman's latest collection of urban poetry. In Baldwin Hills Dom Perignon washed down hot-buttered grits and everyone lived on one of the Dons. That was very important; almost as important as knowing how and when to be a Huxtable.

Fires come and go in Southern California. That's just the nature of the paradise. But the last thing the good black people of Baldwin Hills needed was a too close examination of who they were and why.

Part One

Chapter One

She had had her taste of men. In fact, she had had her *fill* of them. She had been married to the same Lamont Lester-Allegro for some twenty odd years. But her stretch, long and checkered, as a stool warmer at too many hedonistic haunts tailor-made for single black Baldwin Hills bourgies was a smoky testament to her dissatisfaction on the home front. Although her outings usually proved anemic they were frequent enough to cause her older best friend and fellow barfly, Elaine, to jokingly snap-read, "You should get out less."

She couldn't agree more. But she did truly enjoy her addiction to the candy-store view of pretty young black men at bargain time. This was when sophisticated soul sisters—stripped of their ladyisms and armored with their charge cards, condoms, and Slauson Arms motel room keys—pushed and shoved past her to have the dark, fresh, and fleshy goods displayed before them.

It was 1989, spring; maybe summer, and every evening, after her NAACP meetings and Links teas and before her bid whist games with Lydia, Arleta, and Elaine, Maggie Lester-Allegro found herself propped up on her favorite stool at Nuts 'n' Bolts without any awareness of how she got there and no recollection of any prethought in the matter of the vigil. She only knew that she was in automatic drive.

She licked the chilly salt rim of her double margarita and checked out the dim room full of pirates and treasures.

The incongruity of her physical presence among these "other" sisters—baby sisters, pimpled spinsterettes of the happy hour playing in their mothers' high heels, beads, and lipstick, was not lost on her. She smiled in mock deference for she knew that those who filled her immediate surroundings were classes below her in style, looks, and attitude.

She was reminiscent of Diana Ross—all eyes, shoulders, and a hair-weave cascade—and sometimes she seemed to carry herself like some grand mystic bush queen. But more often than not she would slip loosely from her dark, regal stance, like on this occasion as she licked too desperately at the chilly salt rim of her cocktail.

Maggie Lester-Allegro came across like the kind of woman who should have been called by her formal given slave name, Margaret, as in "Oh, Maaaaaahgret daaaaahling!" and she seemed like someone who should have been a heavy frequenter of the old Perino's on Wilshire Boulevard during its heyday back in the 1930s when it was the sacred trough to platinum stars.

But the new piss-elegant Nuts 'n' Bolts in the Baldwin Hills Plaza was where she hung. Hung. Hung drunkenly and conspicuously like some antique drape in a neon setting. Hung. Hung as in "hung around," as in, "Is it time for me to die?"

You see, Maggie Lester-Allegro had long ago resigned herself to her husband's neglect, knowing that she was merely one of his many trophies acquired seasons ago and left upon a dusty mantel of prominence. After all, Lamont Lester-Allegro had family legacy to live up to and personal demons to live down. Lester-Allegros were known for being the first black everything that could be distinguished by being the first black anything in a world that relished firsts. Doctor Lamont Lester-Allegro, a third-generation Lester-Allegro, was known for only that: being a Lester-Allegro, one of no particular distinction, merely a hanger-on by blood.

As Maggie sat at the bar perusing the trade, she recalled with liquor-heavy smirks and moans the night *Queen of Outer Space* played on the Z channel and Lamont insisted on watching it even though HBO was airing *Lady Sings the Blues*. Zsa Zsa over Miss Ross? Oh please! Maggie could only credit the choice to her husband's sense of taste when faced with camp, and yet . . .

"Now that's a real woman!" Lamont had said ogling the TV monitor while a young Zsa Zsa broke English and his proper Negro heart.

Maggie fluffed it off—or seemed to—especially in light of the fact that he had confessed after a night of too much Courvoisier and cocaine that he once let a gorgeous brick-house, during his cum-too-quick college youth, suck him off like some rimmed Tootsie Roll pop. But the drop-dead brick-house turned out to be a drop-dead drag queen with enough dick of her own to hog-tie a judge. So what did he, Lamont, know about a real woman, much less appreciating one? Alas, this was how Miss Maggie Arial Lester-Allegro justified her more-than-occasional pilgrimage to the bar called Nuts 'n' Bolts.

She had ordered another double margarita. Just as Shabaka-Letrice, the waitress, set it down in front of her, she thought she saw Dorian Moore—beautiful Dorian Moore—reflected in the mirror behind the bar. She held back her startle when she realized that the only face staring back at her that she even remotely found of sentimental interest was her own. What she had thought was him was only the recollection of him, a recollection that flashed brightly in her lazy bloodshot eyes.

He was just a boy, a black-as-midnight boy with black-as-midnight eyes surrounded by thick black lashes languid enough and groomed enough to sweep stardust aside. He had sparkling white teeth framed by lips made full enough to tell a thousand lies.

She sipped at her drink and felt a warmth deep down inside that place that made her blank to all that surrounded her vintage self, blank to the music and the madness, the hustlers and the hustled.

She remembered when they first saw each other in the crowded room, like in the song. Lunch hour at Serenity. It was almost a year ago to the day. There he was. Right where Elaine had said he would be. Maggie had been sitting at a preferred table, picking over hot duck salad and dishing the dirt with Elaine, when she looked up and saw him at the bar, his smiling, dimpled blackness sucking her into his unknown. He quite literally took her breath away. She gasped—a tiny little gasp. He saw her see him and he laughed, suddenly, kindly—one of those silent, private laughs. His eyes sparkled with new mystery.

"Well, I think I've stayed too long at the fair," Elaine said with a naughty little victory smile. Then she got up and left, giving the beautiful young man a nod of approval as she passed his way.

Maggie had guessed him to be twenty-one. Maybe. There or about. So she felt flattered and confident in her goods, knowing that she was still lovely and shapely enough for hearty young men half her age. With eyes smiling at her, he got up from the bar and walked slowly toward her table. Her eyes smiled back and invited him to sit.

Magnanimously she allowed him to speak his sweetness and buy her a drink. She pretended to blush when he gave her the detailed directions to his place, which was not far at all, just up Mount Vernon Drive.

She even pretended not to know why she so readily accepted this new chance and adventure, but accept she did. She left the bar ahead of him and pulled herself together with each step; the Diana Ross eyes and shoulders and the hair-weave cascade. By the time the attendant had brought her Mercedes around she was feeling better having pulled it together, knowing that the kindness of a child was hers to do with as she pleased.

Chapter Two

He had lived all his young life nestled in the easiness of L.A. He was a pretty young black thing with few friends but many acquaintances. His sinful good looks, gentle manner, and lip-smacking physique were kept fine, firm, and lean at some nondescript gym and blessed darker than his natural cocoa blackness by long visits to nude beaches. He was the object of sexual admiration and hallowed envy of those who proudly—and with deep innuendo—claimed to know him best.

But he maintained an inoffensive distance, and it was this aloofness free of petty narcissism that kept desire for him kindled in the flaming hearts and stained panties of so many.

Yet he was easy, easy as the city of his birth, easy as the Malibu coves where he so often stretched his naked body, black as rich mahogany on top of beige sand—easy. His own best company. Probably.

He could spend all day in the house alone if he wanted to,

looking out over the city, soaking in a tub, oiled up for masturbation in front of the mirror.

The king of cool out and nonchalance. He probably didn't need the real world as much as the real world needed him.

This was how Maggie Lester-Allegro imagined him, even as she entered the small but stunning cantilevered bungalow with the city-to-ocean view that he called home.

"Well . . . this is it," he mumbled with sleepy charm as he left her standing in the sunken living room while he walked his beautiful bowlegged self to the sliding glass door. The door was the separation of dining area and terrace, a terrace that hovered dramatically over a deep brush-filled canyon that ran next to a descending LaBrea Boulevard. Quite clearly, on a smog-free day, one could see on equal level the Hollywood Hills several miles north.

"Very nice," Maggie found herself saying in a suddenly husky voice, her gaze less keen to the nature beyond the terrace and more attentive to the delectable definition of neatly curved ass hidden beneath white linen pants. He, caught in a moment of environmental religion, stared out over the city below knowing that his back—for her entertainment—was to her. "Very nice," she said again. Only then did he turn to her, slowly, and smile that smile.

"I guess . . . considering what I pay."

"It's really very nice. Very quaint. No, I mean it. It's . . . it's absolutely adorable."

"Thanks."

He stood facing her for a moment longer, looking down at her as she imagined herself melting in the center of his sunken living room, melting under the glare of black-as-midnight eyes that held her transfixed with silent power. Then, and only then, did he move away from the terrace.

It took her a moment, but finally she came to.

"Do you do this often?" She suddenly heard the words slithering past her lips. The earlier margaritas had loosened her tongue's grip.

"Do what?" There was a knowing sparkle in his voice.

"You know . . ."

"No, I'm afraid I don't."

"You know."

"Oh?"

"Do you?"

"Only with the pretty ones."

"Talk your trash," Maggie laughed.

"Have a seat." He gestured with a new kind of stare that almost made her cum.

"Thank you," she said, catching her breath, and then she did so. She sat with an elegant grace and a neat new coyness that conjured ghosts of virgin past.

When he finally asked, "What are you drinking?" it too caught her off guard and suddenly she was grandly indecisive and marvelously confused.

"Anything'll do," she said finally.

"One 'anything'll do.'"

"You need to stop that."

"For lovely Maggie Lester-Allegro."

"You remembered."

"Of course. It's a very lovely name."

"Thank you, Mr. Moore."

"Mr. Moore . . . I love it."

It was the dimples that alerted Maggie, for they made him seem truly young . . . maybe too young for respectability.

Suddenly he was a growing little boy, a flower whose full flourish could be cut short by an impatient admirer choosing to pick without regard for the closed, unblossomed bulb. But his open fragrance that caused a stirring within her, a tingle within her not-bad-for-forty-one-year-old body, demanded guilt to take leave and leave her to the duty of serving desire, serving youth, being served.

She promised herself—even as he fixed their drinks with his back to her, his beautiful ass, a work of high-hoisted, slit-ted perfection beneath white linen pants to her—that she would be gentle with him. Then she laughed, realizing how foolish her Cleopatrian fantasies were becoming. He truly may have been a spring chicken but the sparkle in his eyes told her that he, this deep, dark young thing, had surely danced around the barnyard with more than a few dowager hens while still keeping schoolgirl pussy moist with anticipation that was, she was certain, invariably fulfilled.

"Know how to roll?" The clang of ice cubes being tossed into crystal sang out under his words.

"You mean as in 'rock and roll'?" she asked in her best youthful voice.

"There's some grass on the table."

"Oh hot!"

She admired the many possible herb dispensaries intriguingly laid out before her—a silver cigarette case, a miniature ivory Buddha, an antique snuffbox—while her ears were keen to the sound of liquor splashing against ice in crystal.

Three fat red Thai buds, pungent with their promising funk, awaited her in the antique snuffbox next to the Zigzags. With fragile fingers, she chipped at a bud, then tore off two sheets of cigarette tissue. With concerted, if not effective, effort, she began the ritual of decadent creation. Long, sculpted nails, elegant when holding a brandy snifter or a roach clip, were dismal in this particular effort, offering little assistance.

Without looking up she could sense Dorian coming toward her. She was seated on the sofa—perched, that is—toiling with her assignment when she realized that he was standing so close to her that the discreet hint of his cologne, Royal Bain de Champagne, was in the breeze that entered from the open terrace. His sweet man-child scent swirled about her, flirted with her, fucked with her scandalously. But he just stood there. Yes. Just stood there for a moment, and that was when she looked up, finally, but not high enough, or perhaps as high as she wanted.

It was eyes to crotch.

His eye-level crotch was ever so beautiful and she just could not tell, no, she just could not tell, no . . .

Briefs or boxers? No. It could not have been briefs. No. Not him. No!

Perhaps he hung freely—thick, long, and free. She could not tell. And now as the fantasy danced inside her head, she looked away, back to her rolling drudgery. She needn't let him see her lingering too long on secret treasures. After all, she had dignity to maintain.

He knew how much she needed it—the drink that is—so sweetly he set the lead crystal glass on the table before her and then sat down next to her on the sofa. He then sipped at his own matching drink and sighed with pleasant relief.

"I hope it's all right," he said, leaning back deeply into the womb of the sofa, spreading his long legs into a wide bulging gap, ". . . gin and tonic."

She placed the half-rolled joint to the side with grandeur, picked up the glass, and took a dainty piss-elegant sip.

"Perfecto!" she declared.

"Good," he accepted.

She then set aside the glass and began, with a new naughtiness, the rolling of the joint. Even without looking at him she could feel the warmth of his perfect smile against her neck.

"Thank you for the drink at Serenity," she finally said.

"It was nothing. I only wish it were flowers."

"How very sweet."

"Would you like music?"

"Right now?" she cooed. "That would be wonderful."

When he rose from the sofa she knew. She could tell by the movement as he stood that his generous gift was shielded freely behind white linen, not imprisoned, simply shielded, shielded like the smile of a Muslim East Indian daddy's girl.

As Maggie watched him stroll his bowlegged self across the living room, she felt new warmth that was either relief of tequila and gin locked in congenial intercourse or the flood of sweet memories of days gone by, days when Lamont was not as old and set and careful . . . if such a time ever existed.

Sadness and desire sneaked in and began to conspire within her. She feared that the tongue-loosening liquor would have her mutter something from the heart where the disease of dignity had not yet spread. She would then truly prove to be another too-close-to-over-the-hill girl looking to be fed the lies of a child.

She laughed silently, a tipsy, silent laugh, but did not lift her glazed eyes up off him.

Bring on the lies! she thought to herself as she watched him ease his sweet bowlegged body down to the stereo, down to the altar where, gracefully, he adjusted his frame into a neat, nasty haunch.

All madam could do was stare. And so she did, so hard that she was startled and distracted when the speakers let Luther into the room.

"Oh my," she purred ignominiously, just a tad too much 'tude in her tone, "from one so young I would have expected rap or something with lots of screaming guitars and lyrics with hidden satanic meanings."

He chuckled darkly as he rummaged through his enviable music library, his back still to her, and as the sheer linen pants hugged his thick calves and neatly signatured his hips, she wondered what he tasted like down there.

It had been so many years since Lamont tasted like a schoolboy, when the taste of newly abandoned puberty lingered between his legs and his sweat was an aphrodisiac of sweet young male juices and when, like a mother Siamese, she licked his tight young body clean from nipple to toe, from salad bowl to dick slit.

But then the sag set in. Really? Was it really the sag of soft flesh where once rock-hard pecs and biceps flexed at the very touch of her tongue that now caused her boredom and disinterest? No, it was Lamont.

Yes it was.

Lamont had become bored because Lamont had been spoiled. Yes, that was it. That had to be it.

There was little else left, few unexplored mysteries for him. No new peaks for him in their private world of romance and erotic matrimony. And his disintegrated appreciation for her adventurous service had caused her, many years ago, to let it drift into a disinterest of her own.

And now Maggie Lester-Allegro regretted the wasted years when reciprocation was considered an improper demand from a respectable black woman, even from a respectable black woman who treasured performing unrespectable activities on her husband. She had often wondered if part of her willingness to service Lamont on her knees, on her back, on her stomach like some yard dog bitch, was rooted in all those things she had been taught to believe by her mother regarding the proper place of a black woman under protective slavery to her husband, notions she thought she had abandoned years before disco.

If only, so long ago, at the beginning . . . if only she had demanded reciprocation, equity, perhaps now she would have still commanded Lamont Lester-Allegro's love, sexual desires, and attention.

And if it hadn't been for the child. If only.

Instead she found herself up at the top of Mount Vernon Drive with a boy young enough to be her son who, even if he didn't mean it, had his beautiful high-hoisted ass to her while Luther sang his regrets.

Chapter Three

"So there you are! Girl, how many of those have you had?" Maggie knew she recognized the voice but could not fathom its presence here, so high up in the hills, in the sunken living room; the white linen pants, Dorian, Luther, Lamont, black-as-midnight eyes. But it was all becoming clear to her. Almost clear.

Hazily she looked around, a half-drunken effort to orient herself. Oh yes. Nuts 'n' Bolts. Her favorite stool. Yes, yes. Another double margarita.

Her favorite watering hole. Yes. It had filled, without her noticing, with happy hour pilgrims downing discounted holy water. Come-ons, gossip, updates on Dionne and Johnny's concert at the Greek, head and white women, Ethel and the mayor and their wild lesbian daughter, hummed with a rhythm throughout, punctuated with the occasional burst of laughter and dish-profiling.

The room was so thick with bullshit and smoke rings that Maggie Lester-Allegro was only half sure of where she was.

She knew it was some place familiar though. It felt and smelled like an old friend. And now she knew for sure that she was not in his living room anymore and he was not serenading her in stereo while she, with long, fumbling nails, rolled an eternal joint. No, she was not alone with the black gamma-gorgeous Fagin's boy. Her mind, mellowed by time, tequila, and sentimental trickery, had merely filled its romantic void with a foolish vision of the past that had tried to impersonate the here and now, and almost succeeded.

"Maggie? Are you all right?"

That voice again. Oh yes. Of course, she thought. And then Elaine's face came into focus.

"I think I've had too much to drink," Maggie finally managed to say.

"I'll say you have," Elaine concurred as she lit a Kool filter king. "How many of those have you had?"

"Two . . . maybe three."

"I would hate to have your head in the morning, girlfriend."

The grinning high-yellow Creole with the gap in the middle of his mouth who was sitting next to Maggie got up. Gallantly he gestured to Elaine. She accepted his stool as an offer that was his supreme privilege.

Elaine was a beautiful fifty-year-old only because she believed in her beauty so thoroughly. No one could dispute the empress' new clothes of tasteful, nonapologetic makeup that didn't even attempt to hide what, on a less self-assured woman, would be considered a plain-Jane face of undistinguished features: small, squinty eyes and a skin tone that, on any other woman, would be called baby-shit brown.

But Elaine Ramsey was truly a hot black lady, a real Miss Thing, and she thanked the grinning Creole with characteristic divatude, then turned her back to him with a snap and huddled with her *best* best friend.

"You know it took me forever to get away from Regis? Not that I was in any great rush, I mean, you know. But I'll tell you something. The man had me scratching the ceiling with my toenails. And I know, I know, I'm breaking all the rules of sistah survival—last thing in the world you do is blueprint all your best shit to your best girl—"

"Your fantasies are safe with me."

"Of course they are. I mean, that's what friends are for. I trust you. I just don't trust *him*. Actually I don't trust any of them, not as far as I can throw them. I use them though. I mean, that's what they're for—to use, not to trust. Trust? Paleeze! Cameron was the last man I trusted, God rest his soul, but Regis? He's three legs and a tongue. That's it. And if the tongue goes so do I. I mean, I can't help it if I know what I know. I know men in general and Regis specifically. The moment I'm out of there he'll be hauling up some other bored and lusty Nubian pretender to the throne. But, fuck it, okay? It's all a game anyway, isn't it? I mean, it's them against us, right? And where is that little closet queen of a bartender?"

Maggie may have been drunk but she could still tell that Elaine had snorted a line or three.

"Be nice, Elaine."

"Nice was not the intent."

"You came on to him last week and he turned you down, and that's what has you pissed."

"Honey, any man who doesn't want *this* has got to be a closet queen."

"Sometimes I don't think you like men very much."

"Oh girlfriend stop. I love men . . . in their place.

"And where is their place, might I ask?"

"Wherever I say it is." She took a breath. "When did you become such a champion of the opposition?"

"Opposition or opposite sex?"

"Oh come on now, Miss Maggie, after all these years, don't you know when I'm teasing?"

"That's some awfully bitter tease."

"Hmmm," Elaine assessed, "I think one of us is drunk."

"I'm fine, thank you very much."

"So how's Lamont?"

"Fine," Maggie answered, her voice pitching high with too much defense. Oh of course she had seen him before he left for the office earlier that morning and the previous night had even shared the same bed with him. She did not sleep, but rather lay calmly awake, absently monitoring his routine growls, snores, pauses, twists, turns, and farts. But could she really know him? She pouted within—heaved that is—knowing that her acquaintance with Lamont Lester-Allegro had dissolved ages ago. "He . . . he's fine."

"Liar."

"What?"

"Oh come off the rooftop, Miss Maggie Allegro," Elaine impatiently tisked. "I'll ask you again. How are things between you and Lamont?"

"That's not what you asked before."

"It's not?"

"No, it's not."

"Oh. Then that's what I meant to ask."

"No. What you're trying to do is get me to cosign your vengeful ways."

"Oh no, now, let's just wait, Miss Thing. You have enough vengeful ways of your own to worry about, thank you very much. And another thing. Just because you sit up and play the dowager from *Ebony* magazine, don't tell me you don't get a little itch and 'stank' between them legs, girl."

"My itch and 'stank' salute you."

"Of course they do. They know mamma truth when they hear it."

The bartender arrived not a moment too soon. Elaine was

starving to flirt again so she eyed him up and down with a stare that ate right through his Dockers.

"And whose little boy are you?" she cooed.

"I'm all yours, Mrs. Ramsey." His smile was deferential.

"Good!" Elaine declared. "I want you wrapped. I'll take you home."

And now he laughed, a small laugh of equal respect, "The usual, Mrs. Ramsey?"

"Why are you so mean to me?"

"Oh come on, Mrs. Ramsey, you're way out of my class. I'm still struggling."

"And I'm a struggler's best friend."

"Mrs. Lester-Allegro? Another for you?" he said, turning to Maggie without losing his smile.

"No thank you."

"The things I could do for you," Elaine purred. "I could make you a fortune."

And with a knowing naïveté and a right proper nod, he excused himself and hightailed it back to his station.

"You have no shame," the drunk declared.

"I have no pimples either." Elaine checked out the bartender for the details she had already committed to memory: the baby-face smile and the baby's-breath goatee, the long white-collared neck, the thick Adam's apple that caused his bowtie to dance when he spoke in that naughty-boy baritone, the big ears and size twelves, the print of his dick, long, cut, and thick, down his left inner thigh, the ass built for tonguing. She caught her breath, shook her head, and took a handful of salted nuts from the dish on the bar and popped them into her mouth, one by one.

"Look at him," she continued with a sweet sigh of regret. "Such a fragile little thing, with his pretty young black self. I could use three of him." Elaine then pursed her blood-crimson lips and checked out her face in her Bergdorf compact. With a cocktail napkin she daintily dabbed off the speckles of salt. "You know there's only one way to treat pretty young black men."

"How?" Maggie asked, never but always amazed by anything Elaine Ramsey did or said.

"Well. Always treat them well." Elaine loved how she looked in her mirror. "But always let them know who runs the show. That's why I like the young ones. No matter how they dress, no matter how sophisticated the shit they invariably talk, no matter how good they fuck, they're all just looking to suck their mamma's tit. They coo and they purr and they hiss. They even get a little snotty. But underneath it all they make you feel wanted. They make you feel loved. And even more than that, they make you feel needed. And all you do is kick back and say, 'Its gonna be all right, baby. Mamma's gonna make it so.' That's right. Always let them know who runs the show."

And Elaine Ramsey found herself still staring in the tiny

mirror of her compact, occasionally looking up over it at the boy trade in the bowtie smiling back for a tip. Maggie, eyes bloodshot and nostalgic, marveled at her good girlfriend's brazen technique.

With a piss-elegant lilt and the tiniest of laughs, Elaine dismissed the entire incident and admonition as silly ramblings brought on by that *something* in the air that made Serenity Serenity and divas divine.

Maggie spoke up suddenly to no one in particular. "I can't believe I'm actually out here drinking like a fish, feeling like a tramp, and thinking things that shouldn't be thought."

"Well like I always say," Elaine said, "if you're in denial, stay home."

The bartender arrived just as Elaine was snapping her fingers like a queen and all Maggie could do was think about Dorian Moore. Elaine was busying herself with her drink and her flirting and the awkward stares from the grinning Creole. Maggie smiled secretly. The vision of Dorian Moore danced in her head. Elaine deserved a bonus for that one.

Except for his occasional appearances in her liquor daydreams and her Valium nights, she had not seen Dorian since that one solitary afternoon. And now time begged her to see him again and thank him properly for the memory.

But now, deep into her margarita stupor, she wondered if her growing dependency on good girlfriend advice, frothy booze in an hourglass glass, and respectable drugs was her way of never letting go of the aberration. Fantasy was all she had left of him in her life. That fantasy would have to fill the void, the vacant space that was her life. Perhaps that fantasy was really all she needed on the side: her fix, her fancy, her avocation.

Even Elaine could not understand—would never understand—that that one day, almost a year ago, was sufficient to quench a thirst and that Maggie's clear and present drinking and hanging out at the bar was not an act of desperation—no, not really—but a ritual of religious proportion where mere mortal sex was not needed but not ignored.

The fantasy was as good as the act. She had convinced herself of that. For only in the fantasy could the negligent husband be that serious pretty young black man hot for a not-bad-for-forty-something diva in need.

"How's that joint coming?" he asked in a voice as mellow as the music oozing from the speakers. And it was at that moment that she knew joint rolling was a gift she had been obviously denied.

He was staring at her and smiling. Sheepishly she held up the rumpled tissue cupping crumbled bits of grass. Her eyes begged for alms and he did oblige. To her rescue he came. Slowly. Gently. And her heart, instead of racing, succumbed to the kindness of it all. And her surrender produced tiny beads of sweat on her forehead and neck that gently ignited the fragrance of her perfume, bringing her full womanliness into a new scented being.

"I'm afraid I'm not very good at this," she apologized, more than aware of how closely he sat next to her, giving her a slight case of the willies that felt like good lip-smackin' masturbation.

He then lifted the half-rolled joint out of her hand and she could feel that his hand—his long musicianlike fingers—were as baby-soft as hers.

He licked the rim of the paper with a thick darting tongue that sparkled with lazy independence and dexterity. Then he sealed the tip of the newly formed cigarette with a most generous French kiss. His soft full lips parted like clean, loose foreskin and drew the whole of the susceptible joint between them, and then it was oozed back out. He then held it before him and smiled ever so coolly, pleased with his handiwork.

He looked at her with bedroom eyes of his own, and she felt a tingle, a sudden one, another one, as she pulled herself out of the daze she had fallen comfortably into while watching the ritual of his creation.

She saw the baby-soft fingers holding the joint and floating toward her. Obediently, she pursed her lips, drugged already on his young cool and urging easiness.

The taste of him on the moist joint was fresh and promising. She swallowed hard and waited for fire.

It was a lovely little gold case, a tiny gold vasette that he positioned at the end of the joint which dangled from her begging mouth. The tiny flash of fire crackled, then danced ever so slightly and calmed her naughty heebie-jeebies.

With a God-sent soothing and a longing, she sucked in the smoke, allowing it to daze her brain and warm her body, to pick up where the liquor left off.

She was floating.

She handed him the joint and as she did their eyes met again. His black-as-midnight eyes were unwavering in their friendly stare, even as he took a deep drag and held the smoke trapped inside for an interminable length of time, and then when finally he allowed the smoke to escape and it billowed before his beautiful face and his beautiful eyes, the beautiful eyes stood playfully defiant. The fixed friendly stare was there for good.

They passed the joint back and forth, back and forth, forth and back, until it was gone. And then they sat in silence.

Maggie knew she was high because when he leaned his head back against the sofa and tapped his finger lightly on the cushion to the rhythm of Luther's song, he looked just like her husband, Lamont, and she wanted to cry.

Chapter Four

Maggie was twenty years old when she heard the announcement on her car radio: Martin Luther King Jr. had been shot.

She remembered wailing suddenly, tears obstructing her view and thick traffic eating her alive. She remembered beating the steering wheel with trembling fists, and yelling and screaming and cursing every white man who ever lived.

Through her tears she could barely make out the Avis rental truck crossing in front of her. She was shaking her head and slamming on brakes. She heard herself screaming, tires skidding, car horns blasting. Then there was a sudden, horrible jolt and the crash of breaking glass. There was a heavy pounding in her head and she puckered with a frown at the taste of warm salty wetness in her mouth before everything faded to black.

She could feel herself floating away into an abyss.

In an unstirred darkness she could see herself in a gilded mirror that seemed to be suspended on distinct nothingness.

But no, it was not a mirror, not a reflection. No. It was her, the real her, asleep, pretty, a black sleeping beauty, a twenty-year-old, now going to UCLA, living life and the struggle.

But now it was good-bye. Good-bye to UCLA and the marches and the protests. Good-bye to the brothers and the sisters.

She then felt herself being pulled deeper into the darkness, swept away by a rushing unsympathetic whirlwind with strict schedules to keep. The body of the black sleeping beauty grew smaller and smaller, like a little doll left orphaned on the railroad bench with its fixed Mona Lisa smile that masked confusion, not mystery, while the train pulled away.

She was desperately reaching out from the back of the train, the moving train, reaching out for the little orphaned doll so cold and alone on the railroad bench. But Reverend King, her traveling companion, was holding her back and counseling her to stay on the train and leave the doll: *Yes! Do stay on the train, sweet sepia daughter! Stay on the train and ride with me unto greater glory!*

But twenty-year-old Maggie Arial Simpson, naïve and stupid and spoiled or not, knew herself well enough to know that she had not had her fill of earthly glory. With a new attitude she started pulling away, pulling away from the good Reverend and reaching out with a brand-new fervor, reaching back for the doll, reaching back for UCLA, reaching back for the brothers and the sisters, reaching back for The Supremes and Mamma's macaroni and cheese. She was reaching back for Sadikifu, reaching back for the feel of hard nipples under the spray of brisk morning showers and this week's clearance sale at Saks Wilshire and the presidency of the Marcus Garvey Association. Reaching back.

"No! No! No!"

And then there was a sleepy moan. And then another. And another. Her moans.

Her eyelids seemed to weigh a ton when she tried to lift them. When she finally did, the white heaven surrounded her. And it was stark, muted, and cold as winter rain. Doctor King was standing over her, smiling his angel's smile. He was younger now. Much younger. A little boyish yet strangely stern-handsome. Maggie now had proof that heaven, as had been rumored, truly was the great rejuvenator. He looked fabulous.

"That's much better," he said sweetly. And now, as Maggie stared into his stern-handsome face, she knew that she had escaped the train, had jumped off like Redford and Newman after looting the mail car.

But then it hit her like a ton of bricks. The stern-handsome face was not that of King's. The King had been shot. Shot!

Seeing the new startle and grimness that now filled her eyes, the young doctor with the stern-handsome face bent down to her and stroked her face with professional sympathy. "Get some rest, Maggie," he said gently. She could see a caring in his eyes that tried so hard to be detached. And now she knew for sure. She could see it in the young doctor's eyes; the reflection of her own realization. King was dead.

Dead.

She could not help herself. She started to cry while the young doctor continued to stroke her face.

"Nurse, prepare a half dosage," he said flatly.

"Yes, Doctor Lester-Allegro."

And moments later Maggie's sorrow had dissolved into a chemical Nirvana and all she remembered was the stern-handsome face and the strange musical name, Lester-Allegro.

Maggie Arial Simpson's recovery was swift and successful. Her beautiful face—the doll face—displayed no traces of the accident. The small scars had healed surreptitiously and the only telltale sign of her hospital stay was her obvious school-girl's crush on her handsome and ever attentive physician. And as if designed by romantic oracles with sweet-ending stories, young Doctor Lamont Lester-Allegro found himself equally enchanted by his patient.

Lamont's father, Doctor Abner Lester-Allegro, was moderately pleased and relieved. He concluded that Miss Margaret Arial Simpson would do: not too overwhelming to be distracting, striking enough to dispel rumors.

Joshua and Lahti Simpson were very pleased. Their

daughter had landed a member of one of the most prominent black families in the city. The social hoopla of the union would more than cover up the faux pas of the past.

Yes, Maggie mourning the death of Martin Luther King Jr. was just fine and right proper. But mourning the far less significant death of this Sadikifu Omoro was an embarrassment. Sadikifu was a bothersome radical who wore loud dashikis and had kink-nappy hair, expressed himself with "Black Power" fists held high in the air, spewed subversive ghetto poetry with heathen audacity, and was killed for his trouble almost a month before Maggie's accident. He was shot by UCLA campus police with such Wagnerian élan that the *L.A. Times* ran his picture on the front page. His funeral, featuring an open casket, made the centerfold of *JET*. Fortunately for Joshua and Lahti Simpson a link between Sadikifu and their daughter never appeared in print.

And now the Simpsons religiously courted Doctor Lamont Lester-Allegro, who actually needed little encouragement in his pursuit of Maggie. Maggie, reeling from and disillusioned by the tumultuous events of the previous two months—the loss of a hero, a lover, a cause—had grown sick enough of reality to long for a bit of the dream her parents had always been selling.

It was of no surprise to anyone that she and Lamont Lester-Allegro, after having known each other for such a short time, married with all the pomp and pageantry befitting a refined young lady of Baldwin Hills. Lahti Simpson arranged everything, and with the help of her Eastern Star sisters, pulled off the wedding of the year eight weeks to the day from the proposal.

Reverend James Cleveland's Universal Tabernacle Choir filled the expanse of Ward AME church with a surprisingly subdued and dignified joyful noise. Milton Williams, caterer to the stars, masterminded a reception of gourmet delectables and vintage champagne that bordered on debauchery.

The grand ballroom of the Century Plaza Hotel was filled with ta-ta celebration long after the happy couple had bid their adieus. All Doctor and the new Mrs. Lamont Lester-Allegro wanted to do was stretch out and hold hands as they settled in for the Concorde's takeoff to a two-week honeymoon in Gstaad, where, coincidentally, Lamont would be attending a medical convention.

And it was then and there, all alone in the hotel suite while Lamont golfed with a medical colleague, that Maggie first began to experience the nausea and dizzy spells.

She was not fully certain how she knew, but she knew. She was pregnant with Sadikifu's baby. Sadikifu Omoro had been dead three months—thirteen weeks to be exact—and now his baby was growing inside of her.

The new Mrs. Lamont Lester-Allegro stood in her hotel room steadying herself against the sway of her morning sickness and the wilt of her predicament. She stared out past the terrace where the Alps looked like Sno-Cones. She circled with delicate fingertips the tuck of her navel that hid the growing child while she pondered, worried, debated, and prepared a useless defense.

It was 9:30 A.M. Lamont would be returning from the course at noon. They would lunch at the Café Palazzo de Richet and sightsee before the evening seminar Lamont was sponsored to attend.

At ten past twelve she heard the key in the door. A double martini ordered up from room service had not done the trick.

"Lamont?" she said with a quiver in her voice that alarmed him as he came through the door and that caused him to drop his golf clubs and take her in his arms.

"What's the matter, sweetheart?" He could smell the liquor on her breath. "Are you all right?"

"Lamont, I think . . ."

"What is it, darling?"

". . . I'm pregnant."

"Don't be silly, darling," he laughed as he hugged her in relief. "It's much too soon since we first . . ."

It then hit him while he held her. Her body trembled slightly. His body stiffened. He slowly pulled away from her and stared coldly into eyes that tried desperately to turn away.

"What are you saying to me?"

She closed her eyes tightly and a single tear fell.

"Sit down," he said in a cold, soft tone. She did and he disappeared into the bedroom. Moments later he returned with his medical bag.

"I didn't expect you to be a virgin, but I'm sure as hell not ready for this. Take off your robe."

She did so.

"When was your last period?" he asked as he examined her.

"Two months ago."

He looked up at her.

"I've skipped a month before," she defended quietly. Not another word was spoken by either of them until the exam was over.

"It's too late to do anything about it," he muttered out loud to himself, putting words to an unthinkable thought. "Who's the daddy?" he then demanded.

She told him in a whisper.

"Who?"

"His name is Sadikifu Omoro."

At the Café Palazzo de Richet they ate in steely silence, like death-row convicts having their final meal. That night he stayed out hours past the end of the seminar. When he did finally come in, he climbed quietly into bed next to her, his back to her. She pretended to sleep.

The next morning he gave her medicine for her nausea and said barely a word. They made perfunctory appearances at the convention's social functions and gave requisite performances as the newlywed couple from America.

"We're leaving on Friday," he informed her on Wednesday. And so on their fourth day, the day the medical convention ended and their real honeymoon was to begin, the Lester-Allegros headed back to Los Angeles braced for the rudiments of married life altered from its storybook expectations.

While Maggie unpacked suitcases and vanities in the bedroom of their Don Carlos Drive home she could hear the slight clang of ice cubes. He was downing his third Courvoisier.

"I feel like a total fool," he muttered between gulps while Maggie continued to unpack in silence. "My bride carrying some other niggah's bastard."

"Please don't use that word around me."

"Which word, 'niggah' or 'bastard'?" And then he exploded, suddenly, out of nowhere. And he began to stalk her. "I can't believe this. I just can't believe this!"

With a smoldering of her own she pulled the delicate pieces of silk bed wear from the suitcase with a clawing anger that was the surrogate for words she wanted to unleash in her defense. No matter how stupid the words of explanation sounded as they tumbled inside her like caged animals, she wanted to get them out. She wanted to fight the constricting dry heave of logic that bullied her into silence, would not let her explain the confusion of it all—the irregularity of her menstrual cycle, the deaths, the accident, her total ill-regard for her physical being and her other circus reactions these past weeks while a baby took root inside her neglected body.

He must have read the justification on her face, for in a sudden outburst edging on violence he yelled, "Bullshit!" And then again he yelled it. Again and again: *"Bullshit! Bullshit!"*

And then she heard the glass, the cocktail glass, crashing against the wall. A second later he grabbed her and she was dizzied as he swung her around where they were now facing each other. She was the frightened, defiant child beauty. He was the stupefied ranting fool. She fought that sudden feeling of superiority that had reduced the scene to movie melodrama and felt a need to suppress a laugh. Then real fear overtook her as she was now assured that she was losing—had lost—her mind.

"Were you in love with him?!?" he sneered as if he had discovered a new foul smell.

Her eyes burned into him without waver—defiantly— and he suddenly shuttered as he held her tightly, unaware that her burning eyes were but the mask desperately formed to hide the madness and the confusion in her mind.

Maggie wondered if indeed she did really love Sadikifu, or had she only loved his nobility, his grand-foolery, his anger, and his divine blackness that had turned her parents green with hate and fearful of losing their good "get-along" status. For it was truly his great pride in his blackness—his African-ness, his Negrocentricity—that had first so captured her, even if selfishly, that when she had listened spellbound to the passion and the subversion of his words and had rode buck wild his thick and throbbing manhood, she had felt all at once born gloriously anew.

But did she love him? Truly love him?

"Yes! Yes! YES!!! I LOVE HIM!!!" she lied mammishly.

She gasped but did not flinch nor did she allow a single tear to fall when he grabbed his unpacked suitcase and ran out of the room.

Maggie stood there frozen. She was cracked inside despite the rigidity of her outer frame, her fleshly armor. She stood there until she could no longer hear the roar of his car engine, until the sound had faded away like the sting that now suddenly made her flinch as if she had just been slapped upside her head, had faded away like the prospect of happiness in this new marriage.

She then realized painfully the damage inflicted upon her relationship with her suddenly estranged Lamont. She knew that she had hurt him deeply, cut his manhood to the quick when she had proudly declared that she had loved another warrior from another world and time and for another reason. And she now knew that even as she spoke those words, had spit them in her new husband's face, that she was unsure and regretful.

Sadikifu was gone, yet the fondness that absence was alleged to cultivate had not taken root inside her heart. Not really. It had been blocked by guilt. The simpler man of smaller adventures who had just abandoned her in a state of fury and frustration at retroactive betrayal had now captured her heart's imagination and her pity, and she suddenly loved him—or so she believed.

A barrage of laughter burst forth from her baby-filled belly—belly laughs, deep, stupid, and sailor devilish—and she was now completely sure that she had lost, was losing, what was left of her simple-ass mind, and Lahti Simpson was chanting over and over again in her best colored voice, *Be good to him, baby, be good to him. A good black man is hard to find—hard to find—be good to him, baby, be good to him. A good black man is hard to find—hard to find.*

It was Maggie's mother's voice, that good old colored Pearl Bailey voice from that good old colored past, from generations of slavery, docility, and watching her men being circumcised at the nuts while dangling from the tree of Emmett Till. Her mother's voice haunted her throughout the long vigil that was her husband's absence, a week to be exact.

She knew that Sadikifu had not died in vain. No. He had died to give new life to proper pursuits. She felt grateful to him for what he had left, a legacy that permitted her to get a piece of the dream, to be a part of the fantasy, no matter how fucked up it was. She was positioned, in everyone's eyes, correctly. She could live the hassle-free life as Mrs. Lamont Lester-Allegro, the doctor's wife. And Sadikifu, neither his nobility nor his heir, could stand in the way of what his death had given her.

Bullshit! Bullshit!

She was confused for seven days, throughout the full term of her husband's estrangement. She was confused and lost, torn between two ghosts, two teachers who had given their lessons and then moved on to other ground, away from her.

Suddenly she began to mourn the selfishness that her heart and mind aspired to in the name of weakness and despair. She became the good widow, just like Mamma Simpson had carefully taught her. And she was a *good* good widow, waiting for her dead husband to rise from the grave like Lazarus, like sweet Jesus on the third day. She would be waiting for him in her new Easter mind and she would 'fess up to her sins and beg for his forgiveness and seek salvation through him.

Her mind was going, going, going . . .

And so when finally, after seven days, Doctor Lamont Lester-Allegro returned to his damaged merchandise, she vowed to give the baby away and he swore to love her for the rest of his life.

As weeks passed Maggie got bigger and bigger. The Baldwin Hills gentry, particularly Abner Lester-Allegro, was deliriously primed for a new Lester-Allegro heir. Lamont and Maggie knew an explanation would have to be concocted and carefully presented. Friends, family, and social acquaintances could not be allowed to feel cheated when told the smooth cover-up that Maggie had delivered prematurely and the baby had died.

And so that's how it went. The concerned were informed of the sad outcome through reports delivered from seclusion. The community was now allowed to mourn in their best Ward AME fashion the unseen corpse of the stillborn child. The item was covered in both the Church and Society sections of the *L.A. Sentinel* and received another two hundred words in Gertrude Gipson's column. The lie had been so well played that even Maggie began to believe the death.

But during the moments—and they were frequent— when she came to grips with the truth, she cried inside, privately mourned the loss of her baby, not to death, but to the discreet services of a highly reputable adoption agency in the South Bay Area.

If only she had not asked to see him. If only Lamont had said no. But both of them were many, many things: a wife full of guilt, a mother-to-be, a woman; a physician with all the attendant compassion, a husband pained by his own inadequacies seen and not seen, a man.

Lamont stood by quietly in the private delivery room of the small Palo Alto hospital while the unfamiliar but reputable small-town doctor, Rueben Alexander, who was unaware that Lamont himself was a doctor, supervised Maggie's easy but difficult birth. Lamont's emotional predicament caused him to silently heave in the process. Ambivalence battled the depths of despair and the heights of elation. And Maggie knew this. She could see it in him. She could see him breaking down and wanting to back away from the decision she had made for the both of them. She could see that small glimmer of hope in him: that they could keep the baby.

But no. That could not be. The existence of this child in their lives would be a constant reminder to Lamont of what he was not and, perhaps, could never be. It would remind her of the same.

Sadikifu was dead. All things reminiscent of him must die away too if there was to be a chance for them, Maggie and Lamont, and happiness.

In spite of the natural pain that comes with childbirth, Maggie barely cried out; the painful thoughts far outweighed the physical discomfort. Dutifully—absently—she followed Doctor Alexander's encouraging commands while nurses assisted like ladies-in-waiting.

The child, a boy, was born perfect. And during the few moments after, when the excruciating pain of delivery gives way to the unfathomable joy of new life and new motherhood, Maggie, without thinking, just feeling, reached out to the sweet cries of her child, stunned by the physician's slap into taking his first breath, and all she could say was "please."

Lamont's eyes said it all. And the newly cleaned baby he could not bear to look at was put in its mother's arms.

Though she was too weak to cry, Maggie was strong enough to hold her son. And she kissed him all over and examined him all over, wanting but not wanting to photograph everything about him in her mind, in her heart: his little yawning smile that said he knew just who she was, dark sparkling eyes strangely open and wide, the smooth baby skin of smoky gold that seemed to grow darker, deeper, even as she held him in her arms, and the tiny little birthmarks—near-matching teardrops—barely noticeable within the lower fold on his left inner thigh.

She then looked up at Lamont. Having stolen a glance, he could now only turn away. The delivering physician and his staff of ladies-in-waiting were too routinely pleased by the everyday miracle to notice the ignominy.

To be given away. To be given away. Maggie thought about it over and over until she could handle it no more. Tears began to fall, tears that matched the matching tears that marked her baby's birth. A nurse, understanding a new mother's state yet not knowing this mother's plan, smiled and gently removed the child from his mother's trembling arms.

"Now don't you fret," the nurse cooed sweetly. "You'll have a lifetime to be together."

And so as that episode in her life—their lives—became more and more distanced, Maggie tried to forget. She knew that she had to forget that there was a child, forget the dizzy spells and confessions made in a Swiss hotel room. She had to forget the schoolgirl daydreams and be the woman whom he needed as much as he needed the diplomas on the wall.

She had only to remember her mother's admonitions, those philosophies that seemed to keep her so happy. Well, at least contained.

And so the honeymoon, delayed by things forgotten and forgiven, had begun anew, not in some foreign country but in the bedroom of a Baldwin Hills home where a stern-handsome young doctor, prince of darkness and his perfect and pedigreed wife, fell winsomely victim to new love and lust.

Margaret Arial Lester-Allegro, fueled by guilt and gratitude, schooled by one who had held on to her own man—her mother—learned to please her old man in the old-fashioned way.

Give him what he wants and he will not venture far, if at all.

Maggie faced her hesitation head-on and dived into what she thought she had to do. She shivered at the touch of his lubricated nine inches kissing playfully at the tight lips of her virgin ass. She moaned with brave delight, for her puckered rectum was not wrecked at all. It was fed bountifully and smiled wide for more, thrilled with him filling it, easily, warmly, thickly, ruthlessly.

She gave it all to him. Everything. All of her bad and guilty self. She wanted to, needed to, for he could disappear out of her life just as easily as he had appeared.

As time went on she gave him more and more: spankings with spiked leather, golden showers, handcuffs and torture racks, anything she thought he might want. But he soon became bored with the games and the punishment, and he truly did begin to disappear.

When this happened, Maggie was somewhat surprised that she did not get any crazier than she was, surprised at how well she was able to pretend that it did not matter anymore. No, not anymore. She pretended not to hurt so much when he was gone—still there and gone. She just didn't give a damn anymore. She was determined to convince herself of that, just as she was determined to convince herself that none of the losses, none of them—not Martin, not Sadikifu, not that sweet baby boy, not even her sense of self—mattered anymore.

"Maggie?"

But she could not answer. Not right now.

"Maggie," Elaine nudged her, "you're crying in your margarita."

"Wha . . . what?"

"You're coming apart, girlfriend."

"Am I?"

"Your makeup is running."

"Is it?"

"You won't be in any shape for cards like this."

"Sorry, Mamma . . . I'm sorry."

Chapter Five

"No driving, girlfriend. And you know Lydia and Arleta are going to be so pissed when they see you like this, out in public and all. You can pick up your car tomorrow."

Elaine figured that the grinning Creole who had earlier offered his bar stool and who had been hovering in her general space all evening had earned the honor of helping her drunken friend to the car.

Elaine prided herself in being Maggie Arial Lester-Allegro's *best* best friend. Maggie Arial Lester-Allegro had a certain thing about her—a something—that made the most skeptical believe she had diamond class, which she did, and not even this drunken exit, this sleazy blow against her iridescent dignity, could tarnish her rep.

Begrudgingly Elaine admired her. Begrudgingly. Yes.

Elaine tisked to herself and allowed herself to be distracted by the grinning Creole's slimy dexterity—awkwardly holding the passenger door open as Maggie elegantly stumbled in, handing Elaine a blue laminated gold-lettered personal business card, and yet somehow managing to grab a good clawful of her ample behind.

"Now, now," she purred as she circled defensively to the driver's side. She aimed a coquettish little wave and threw a plastic little smooch at the high-yellow Cheshire, then hopped in and sped the car away.

"Why do I attract all the circus acts?" she sighed dramatically.

But Maggie did not hear her. No. Maggie Arial Lester-Allegro allowed herself to float away on memories of Dorian Moore where Luther sang of here and now.

"My God you're gorgeous," she remembered saying accidentally when he innocently stretched in front of her. "Oh. I'm . . . I'm sorry," she continued with a gasp—high off Thai stick, Bombay gin, and desire. "I didn't mean that. I mean, I did, but what I really meant was . . . Oh God . . . you know this is really some tongue-loosening smoke, and you know what they say, 'loose lips . . . ' "

". . . make for great lovemaking," he said with a smile worth licking.

She could only stare back at him, touched by that charming little turn of a phrase ". . . make for great lovemaking." It suddenly seemed like an offer that went beyond mere sex. Was it truly an offer of love, no matter how brief? Or was she just tripping?

Silently, sadly, gratefully, she was being carried away by her own crazed thoughts—thoughts of him, thoughts of Lamont—and those thoughts began to threaten her already fragile mind.

But even if she were crazy as a loon, she was not blind. She knew Nirvana when it surrounded her. Lamont was the old pain and Dorian was the newfound pleasure—her pretty young black thang—and yes, she was tripping, trippin' hard. But why not? She believed that she was entitled.

"How's your drink?" he mumbled with intent.

"Oh God, I'm on empty," she Betty Booped back.

He took her glass and sauntered over to the bar.

"And could you check the oil while you're at it?" She knew she was being bad but she just couldn't help herself. He rewarded her audacity with a growl and then turned his back to her while he freshened her drink.

"You have a very nice ass," she declared.

"So I've been told."

You're a model," she went on.

"Really?" he replied.

"It's in the walk," she pronounced.

"I'm a painter," he then said.

"Well . . . okay," she conceded, taking the glass. "Are any of these yours?"

He looked around the room and at each wall where the

dark divas—La Baker, Miss Lena and Ross—hung enshrined in oil and charcoal, on film and canvas. Then he looked back at Maggie with eyes that saw inside her dirty mind.

"No," he said, "these are just good prints of other people's work, a few originals, things like that. I sell all mine."

"You must be very good."

"I make a living."

"I see."

And suddenly it was happening. He was kissing her, so sweetly, so gently, that it took her breath away. She then pulled back, ever so slightly, in fear of an ecstasy that kills, and then she turned away from him, savoring the sweet taste of his soft thick lips thrilling her beyond repair.

"How did you know?" she managed to ask.

"I read lips."

He touched her face with a single finger which brought her 'round into his stare. He was so pretty, so nice and young and black and pretty. And his pretty young black finger toyed with the pucker of her lips, lips too loose to resist flirtation. And so they gave in, they surrendered and parted obediently, but ever so slightly, just enough to let her tongue stroke and probe a part of him—a pretty black finger, a much needed warmth, a reaching out, a little care.

But before she could taste it all, locks were unlocking and door chains were calling her name.

Chapter Six

"Drunk!" Lydia declared at the first glance of Maggie pouring through the front door of their house on Don Thomaso Drive.

"Again!" Arleta concurred, shaking her head as she steered them all toward their game room.

Lydia Titus was beyond in love. She was absolutely fortified by her seventeen-year committed relationship to Arleta Moorehouse Grey of the Detroit Greys, fast-food people who, years earlier, had turned old slave dishes into an eight figure annual gross income through a nationwide chain of soul food drive-thrus. The Greys of Detroit were right up there with Cosby, Oprah, and the two Johnson clans.

Arleta Moorehouse Grey was a bright young thing, a fabulous forty-year-old silly-willy of a child whose purple beauty was equal to that of her longtime companion. To see Lydia and Arleta together made it easy to see the depth of their love and romance. They also had a felineship based on an intriguing mix of vanity and self-esteem. They needed only to glance at each other to glance at themselves. They were dark Double-mint twins whose very startling presence evoked a crystal-framed mirror image.

Though a sepia dilettante of monied leisure in many harm-less ways, Arleta was not unmoved by Lydia's fierce by-the-bootstraps savoir faire. The fact was she admired it as long as it did not get in the way of good times, great parties, and those wonderful sojourns to the white beach that fronted their twelve-room cottage on Grand Bahama Island.

Judge Lydia Titus was often called Judge "Tight-ass" by nervous public defenders, fat-off-the-crime private coun-selors, and politically ambitious worker bees—assistant D.A.s, three-piece lackeys, and assorted bureaucratic ass-lickers—who brought their honey to her throne, for they had been warned by many who had tried that she didn't fuck around.

But if Her Honor had an Achilles' heel it was her deep pas-sion for her lady and her deep passion for her cards.

Bid whist.

She was indeed addicted to the game and most likely fell in love with Arleta Moorehouse Grey seventeen years earlier to some degree because in her she had found a life mate who lived and breathed six nos, Bostons, and trump-fat kitties as much as she did.

Arleta Moorehouse Grey, Lydia Titus, Elaine Ramsey, and Margaret Arial Lester-Allegro made the perfect four-some—black bourgeois sorority sisters of a not-so-unusual

Southern California ilk drenched in quiet power, patience, passion, and long-suffering. Explosions, like land minds, waiting to happen at the most unsuspecting time.

The four best friends got down to immediate business—bid whist.

Maggie neither sobered up nor got drunker. She simply *woooooooozed* in a holding pattern, a purgatory of inherent dignity, of cotillion class bravely held up against falling-down drunkenness. She was a trooper, for the moment, a credit to her piss-elegance and saddityhood. And so she stayed oiled between the cracks, allowing only so much of that night—Lamont's slipped confession of boredom the night *Queen of Outer Space* played on the Z channel and Miss Ross played on HBO—to intrude upon the game. It was bid whist night. Bid whist. Whist à la cart.

"Four."

"Five."

"Six low."

"Six no. Downtown."

Arleta lit a joint to calm the nerves she pretended to have in need of calming. Miss Elaine had taken out her bid with a "no trump," and Arleta was sportingly pissed, which made Lydia howl and snap her fingers, being able to tell by her lover and partner's dramatic display that Arleta and her bid were doomed. Of course all of this meant that no one really noticed that the mind of Maggie Lester-Allegro had slipped passed her vow, had crept back up the warm breezes of the past to the memory of a boy.

The smell of him. That's where she was. The lemon pungency of his youth on that late afternoon had dizzied her and weakened her and reduced her to a youthfulness of her own and a foolishness well deserved.

Yes. She was back to being that schoolgirl again, that little Miss "It," Mount Vernon Junior High School's black Barbie doll the year they shot John Kennedy, the first time she sucked Sadikifu's dick when his name was Raymond Harris Jr.

No! No. Not that far back. Too far. TOO FAR!!!

No . . .

It was just last year. Yes. Almost a year to the day. No. Not Sadikifu. Dorian.

Sweet Dorian Moore.

He kissed her again and she almost drowned, but then with a suddenness she came up for air, cleansed by the baptism of his gentle touch.

Then suddenly she began to laugh and he pretended not to know why. He just smiled that smile, gave her dimples and black-as-midnight eyes, and moaned a dreamy "What?"

"You have lipstick on," she giggled.

"Oh?" he asked innocently.

"My color looks good on you," she teased.

"Really?" he flirted back.

"You'd make a beautiful girl," she prissied.

"Is that a fact?"

And she was ready to lick his pussy.

But instead she fetched her purse—yes "fetched" it—and proceeded to ease him down next to her on the sofa. Then, for some strange reason, she felt like Ethel Waters mammying the little white girl in *The Member of the Wedding*.

Switch reels, she ordered herself in silence.

"I have a Kleenex in here somewhere," she singsonged, cautiously rummaging through her Gucci, afraid of what she might reveal. "Ah! Here we are . . . you don't mind, do you?" she asked, having already aimed the Kleenex toward those lips.

"By all means," he mumbled easily, moving in and to her, giving her all of his beautiful face. Ever so slightly he puckered his lips and his eyes closed. His thick long lashes almost touched his cheeks.

A calm, almost religious, held her frozen in a stare. He was so perfectly beautiful she almost shed a tear. The hand that held the Kleenex meant to wipe his lips trembled. Between her legs a drop of moisture tingled. She squirmed a bit, in a way that let him know she was ripe, weak, and sticky.

She tried to pull herself together but could not. Not completely.

With strokes wrought with innuendo she wiped and

dabbed at juicy lips; wiped and dabbed . . . wiped and dabbed . . . dabbed and wiped until they were lip-smacking clean.

"Oh! Where was I?" She snapped out of it.

"Are you playing or not?"

"Yes . . . yes . . . yes."

"Miss Thing to Earth. Miss Thing to Earth."

"Come on, girl, we know you have the ace."

And she did, so she played it and took the book.

It was after midnight—four full hours of nonstop play— before someone called it quits (it certainly was not one of the dark Doublemint twins), and they all found themselves laid out on chaise barges, sipping brandy and coffee, and watching silent videos of boys fucking boys.

After a long, still quiet, Elaine burped—a dainty little ladylike burp—and then for no particular reason she just started talking while a new something young, black, and pretty gave it his all onscreen.

"Sex and coffee," Elaine said out of nowhere to no one in particular. "Cameron on the j-o-b. That man would have me in seventh heaven, all lost up in the nasty, and then came those first few drops of something hot and delicious like fudge on vanilla ice cream—a shutter, a gasp, a moan, and I would feel dizzy and dazed like I couldn't hold my balance even though I knew I was lying down.

"Cameron on the j-o-b. And then my eyes would open and before I could think, Where am I? I would still feel myself all caught up in the nasty. And there he'd be, his beautiful spit-shining premature bald head bobbing up and down between my legs with a smacking, him having his good-morning pussy. His darting tongue killing me with pleasure. So each morning of my married life prior to this young widowhood, I just went on and died a thousand deaths of pleasure. For twelve years—every day, at the break of dawn, come rain or shine—he'd feast on me, then he'd fuck me. And I mean he'd fuck me good. He'd fuck me till my nose bled. And then we'd have coffee."

"Nothing beats good head."

"Truly."

"I am sooooo high."

"Truly."

"Speaking of coffee."

"Yes."

"Yes."

"Maggie?"

"You know she needs it."

"You know that's right."

"Look at her. She looks so peaceful all curled up there."

"Bullshit. She looks like she's having a wet dream."

"Oh please, Elaine, little boys have wet dreams."

"Oh please yourself. I had them all the time as a blossoming teen. I guess I should've considered myself blessed but you know how teenagers are, don't miss it till it's gone. I used to be able to cum just like that, in a snap. Thank God Cameron came along, with his good head-giving self. And twenty-seven-year-old Regis is not bad either. I mean, he's no Cameron, but his young tongue knows its way around the pink hole, much thanks to my diligent tutelage, which I'm sure the little son-of-a-bitch is using on some of these other old divas of the Hills. But I just can't help myself. I like the young ones. I married Cameron when he was young. Right out of his teens. Yes. Just call me Robin Hood. I rob the cradle to feed the old."

Maggie, who had remained silent and distant throughout was truly not one to taunt, not at this moment, not while she half slept, half listened and fully kept caught up in the web of a pretty young black man who made her day one lovely afternoon almost a year ago. She could not put it into words but was glad Elaine could express her matching sentiments so eloquently and right on target.

Nothing like them. Nothing. No. Not a thing.

Not when they're young and sweet and adventurous, and so eager to please, when they still have dreams to reach for and kingdoms to conquer instead of lying back inattentive to the passion because privilege, position, and prosperity cushion their fall toward life and the pursuit of living. She needed a Dorian in her life. She needed him like a cool drink and a kind word. Like a swing out on a veranda. Like Doctor Feelgood. She needed him, and was grateful to have had a taste of him, a taste of his young self, the lingering aftertaste of too sweet Kool-Aid and too sweet boy.

Needed him. Needed his perfection. His perfect self.

"Make love to me? Not just sex?"

"Don't worry, lovely Margaret Arial Lester-Allegro. I come with a money-back guarantee."

And she knew he meant it. And she knew that he was going to be worth every penny of his thousand dollar fee.

"Shall I pay you now . . ." she almost begged, ". . . or after?"

"That's not important," he said so simply, so tenderly. "Anytime is fine. Before. After. Anytime you want."

And she could now only look at him with a monumental gratitude, and she fought hard to hold back the tears of joy.

"Anytime *I* want," she could hear herself saying with a newfound calm. "You don't know what that means to me. Anytime I want. My wants. Oh God . . . I'm so ready to be loved right now. And here you are. Ready to venture where no man dared to go. Yes. I think I'll pay you now."

Chapter Seven

The discovery of the dead blonde—her name was Mercy Randolph—on the Lester-Allegros' doorstep was truth stranger than fiction. The story, in its various interpretations, strode scandalously through Baldwin Hills, inciting praise, condemnation, and much finger snapping.

Blue-haired dowagers huddled in back pews, "girled" each other in nail salons, and conference-called their Eastern Star cronies all up and down the coast while feigning deep sympathy for the terribly wronged Mrs. Lester-Allegro. And such a pretty thing for her age.

When the truth behind the melodrama was revealed, the celebrity of the tale took on new proportion and endured full strength for several months.

Maggie was in the pool when she heard the shot. It was a hot day—muggier than Southern California had a right to be—and the Santa Anas were feverish. Maggie desperately needed a dip.

Elois Andrews across the street must have been the first to

see the dead white woman, or if not, was at least the first to scream. Leisured down by margaritas, Maggie slipped out of the pool and very slowly headed for the house. The whole neighborhood had converged outside the low shrubbery that walled her lavish property before she even noticed.

She swung wide her front door and while her neighbors oohed and ahhed with proper black upper-middle-class reserve, she knew that they all knew what she now knew.

Francine Harvey from next door truly did not have to take the note from the dead woman's cleavage; after all, she didn't die on *her* doorstep. But she did, she did take the note. And Yula Tyson didn't have to take the note from Francine and read it out loud, but she did. Miss Yula Tyson was that kind of woman.

Lamont,
It's been more than three years. I can't share you anymore. I'm leaving you the only way I know how.

                                        Mercy

Needless to say Mrs. Maggie Arial Lester-Allegro was outdone. Here was some blond bitch with half her brains splattered all over her front steps and a written record of her husband's Zsa Zsaesque infidelities, on top of wretched Santa Ana winds. How could anyone blame her if she seemed to be going a little crazy?

Arleta didn't blame her. Lydia didn't blame her. Elaine

didn't blame her. They all sort of . . . understood. Besides, it was so long ago and Maggie seemed to be all right now, and Lamont had truly made great strides in bringing some civility, if not sex and sympathy, to a relationship and a marriage laid in a ditch and left for dead.

But fuck all that. What is that anyway? What does any of it have to do with anything anyway? What's wrong with a little break-away bullshit and a little bid whist with the girls and a little reminiscing about a good time with a young boy? Even if such remembrances stayed in the head, stayed in the heart, kept a safe distance from the uglier and unspeakable outcome?

You get what you pay for. That she truly knew. And if that was what he cost than that was what she paid. A small price indeed. And besides, he came with a money-back guarantee. What more could a woman in her state of mind want or need?

So then where did the madness come from?

How could she have gone off and done what she had done, or had thought she'd done? She had gone stark-raving mad somehow. She thought she knew what it was. She thought it was a loud kind of madness heard 'round the world, a madness going down for the third time, flailing arms and chopped-up pieces of desperate silent screams, piercing even as they die in gulps. She thought it was the kind of madness only someone like herself could have conjured up with such deadly, painful accuracy.

No. Grand is not always easy!

Chapter Eight

Albee Mention—whose given name was Ralph Chester-
field, a name abandoned during the 1960s renaissance for
the moniker Ali Muhammad, which he later surrendered,
when Disco lobotomized the movement in the mid-1970s, for
Albee Mention (he was and always had been a closet fan of Ed-
ward Albee)—was a serious writer of blaxploitation.

His books, whose covers were inspired by velvet paintings
of earthy lovemaking dramatized by black lighting, were
prominently displayed between the Harlequin romances and
the collected works of Iceberg Slim at every Kmart in every
black and fashionably liberal Jewish neighborhood across the
country.

Turning out five to ten titles a year, he raked in the money
and, wearing his wealth like too much cologne, did often look
like a fur-collared pimp from the 1970s. He was often stopped
by Glendale police who were first alerted by the color of his
skin, which caused them to take particular note of the heavily
detailed metallic Rolls, and then felt confirmed in their Aryan

suspicions upon closer inspection of the caricature behind the wheel.

Most of the cotillion elite of Baldwin Hills, on the other hand, tried to ignore the existence of their dubiously monied neighbor who was also housed on the back shelves of Kahlila's Book Emporium next door to Marla Gibbs' theater and across the street from Leimert Park. That is, the books were housed there, not the author, who lived palatially at the summit that was Angeles Vista Boulevard and Don Carlos Drive, across the street from Doctor and Mrs. Lamont Lester-Allegro.

Albee Mention and Lamont Lester-Allegro were the very best of friends and no one could really figure out why.

They had often crossed paths with no more than cordial nods across Don Carlos Drive—the Lester-Allegros on the even side of the street, the Mentions on the odd—on those days when "true" members of the clubhouse and monied wannabes had no choice but to cross each other's paths: the early morning routine of putting out the cans on garbage day when the housekeeper was off; the occasional earthquake strong enough to make both the conspicuously grand and the quiet elite run out whooping in the streets like the sanctified caught up in thinking that this one was the BIG one; and watering one's own lawn on those days when the gardener thought the sun was too hot for anything but the beach. Yes, they had crossed paths with cordial nods, but they had not really spoken. Not until Glendale. There was no need to before then.

"Brothaman," Albee would chime in a smooth baritone that did not seem to fit him. That's how he always referred to Lamont—Brothaman, and he, all six feet four inches of him, was known to bury the smaller man—Lamont stood at a lean and even six feet, a hundred and seventy-something tight cut pounds—in a roughhouse bear hug whenever they met, which was often.

They hung out like schoolboys playing hooky, which sometimes caused the more traditional Lamont to flinch with guilt and sneakiness. Albee Mention, on the other hand, did not suffer such fantasies of career self-flagellation, for although he was astonishingly prolific, he was self-described as "lazy as fuck." He simply did not subscribe to the notion of suffering for the art and only wrote when he truly felt like it. Even then, he only wrote in small spurts—a paragraph here, twenty minutes there. But somehow books got written, published, and bought. Therefore no reason existed to discourage his leisurely ways.

Lamont Lester-Allegro and Albee Mention. They were really quite a unique pair, these two. They were successful black men who seemed to have it all, had learned the game and played it well, and had all the trinkets and trappings to prove it—the right kind of houses in the right kind of neighborhood with the right kind of wives.

Vera Mention was an as-white-as-you-can-get home girl from Breedlow, Texas. Albee had picked her up during a weekend in Vegas. He had mistakenly accused her of picking his pocket after she fucked him sore at Caesars. After his Epsom salt bath that night he took her to an expensive dinner as a show of apology, then married her six weeks later.

Vera Mention and Maggie Arial Lester-Allegro did not hang out, no, not at all. As far as Maggie was concerned there was already one too many Great White Hopes, too many young Zsa Zsa's within shot of her husband's nine inches. She knew what they were and she knew what they stood for. No matter what shape they were in. Old or tired or broken or fat or whorish or cheap or all of the above. They were still "in." They were *always* "in." They were still aspirations. They were still goals. They were still high-water marks for some, acts of vengeance for others, and a pounding on the chest, a grabbing of the balls, and a screaming from the lungs "I am a man!" for still far too many. Still, in these so-called progressive 1980s.

So it was strange—or maybe not so strange at all—that the denouement which brought onstage all the principal players—Maggie, Elaine, Dorian, Lamont, Albee, Vera, and Mercy—would be played out with so much blood and madness and melodrama.

But it all went back to Glendale, and years earlier, back to Breedlow, that lower Texas pass-through for itinerants headed for California's mostly mythic, rarely realized, celluloid gold.

—⊶∞⊶—

Herb Rooney and his wife, Della, were the proud white trash pillars of Breedlow, Texas. But soon the lure of Hollywood was too much to resist. They pulled up stakes, packed up their daughters, and made the move. Herb landed a security guard job at 20th Century–Fox while Della became a union extra who got plenty of work through Central Casting and Universal Studios.

Herb was also a staunch supporter of the "protectionist" school and was not about to see his beautiful blond, blue-eyed daughters, Vera and Mercy, become "nigger fodder." He often preached the gospel of racial purity and thought he had reared them in the correct and righteous ways of his ancestors with incredible tales of the black man's evil. But that only served to intrigue his young, juicy, bouncing, blond babies much like the fruit on the Lord's Tree of the Knowledge of Good and Evil tempted. It was all in the last name: Evil.

When Vera and Mercy would overhear their father's tales of how Grandpappy used to cut off the fat dicks of pretty young black men after they were lynched, the girls wanted to know why the fat dicks of pretty young black men had to be cut off. What was so fearful or loathsome or nasty about them? What was so wonderful about them?

It was this question that initiated the search.

Chapter Nine

"Slap me again and I'll chew your mothafuckin' knuckles off, you black motherfucker!" Mercy screamed at Joe Jay Randolph. Furiously, she picked herself up off the floor and brushed away the disheveled blond hair that now covered her face like snarled, dull Christmas tinsel. Then she wiped at the mascara-stained tears that streamed down her red-bruised cheek and got right up in Joe Jay Randolph's face again. So Joe Jay Randolph slapped her again just to see if she would chew his mothafuckin' knuckles off.

"BITCH!" he yelled, like she had hit *him*. And then she kept her word. She snagged his hand in her mouth and bit down with everything she had. The pain sent a bolt right down his spine and between his legs his balls tightened like frozen prunes.

He was howling now, howling like a dog on fire. He danced around the room with his vicious wife dead tight on his bleeding hand. He knocked at her and knocked at her and knocked at her, and kept on howling and dancing her around.

But the grip never loosened. He then danced her over to the window and threw her through the glass. Blood was everywhere: her blood, his blood. So she bit deeper, and now he was crying and wailing so bad that he never even heard the police break down the door.

They beat the shit out of him. Literally. They beat him so bad that he shitted all over himself. And as batons slammed on every part of him—his back, his stomach, his kneecaps, and rib cage, on his head, in his face—he almost wanted to laugh, laugh at the weird sound of cracking bones and squishy bloodletting.

When he woke up he was in a hospital bed and a man with a thin grin was looming over him.

"Joe Jay, welcome back," the man said, his breath bad enough to cut through the smell of medicine and rubbing alcohol. "I'm Frank, your lawyer."

The story of the Joe Jay Randolph beating, videotaped through the motel's snoop and security system, hit the evening news on all four networks and stayed front page for the full two weeks Joe Jay lay unconscious.

The city was in an uproar and the mayor had a plan. After all, this was still Hollywood.

From sea to shining sea the country held its breath and, while still bloated up, prayed diligently for that poor black man beaten up by L.A.'s finest.

Four police officers, three councilmen, two commissioners, one police chief, and 8.5 million dollars later, Joe Jay Randolph was back on his feet and feeling good as new.

Even things between him and his wife, Mercy, were a lot better. (Who says money can't buy you love?) She nursed him and babied him like she used to do in the beginning, when she called herself over with being this trashy little white girl from Breedlow, Texas, who once sucked some man's dick because he made her believe that he was Wesley Snipes.

Joe Jay was really her kind of pretty young black man: old enough to know better and young enough to not give a damn. He was a dick and a fist, now a rich dick and a fist. And Mercy took it as long as she could. She loved getting fucked and fucked up by him—until one day when she remembered the privilege she bore by the tint of her skin.

If there was nothing else, there was one thing she learned from her father. She was a white woman in a white world. And although she had miles to go to reach a white man's status, she was still his prize, his cause, and, cocooned in the preciousness of her gilded and fanciful cage, miles above the black men she so desperately craved.

But there was sweet danger in the dark. It was in the dark that desires were fulfilled: pussies were licked good and fucked sore, and titty nipples were nibbled and pinched with the pleasures of pain.

Just the very thought of the danger in the dark would make her cum, just like the thought of the danger in the dark had put the fear of God in the "goodest" of good white Christians and pink-back, flat-bottom white boys who fucked with a purpose but not with a passion.

But now the danger in the dark that lived within Joe Jay was now becoming a one-trick pony. The fucking and the fucking up, the dick-then-the-fist was becoming a mundane routine. And like the good white woman that she knew she was, she knew that it would be easy to move out and move on and still find the darkness that sought out the light.

Her brother-in-law, Albee, knew what she wanted, but when asked by her, now a cash-rich divorcée in search of some struggling young black man, to make the hookup, she was more than surprised and somewhat disappointed to be introduced to this bourgeois doctor who was whiter than she.

True, he was dark as the blue-black abyss, but he carried himself like a dickless white man, straight up and swaggerless. Yes, where was that swagger which was supported by bowlegs made bowed by the sway and the weight of thick, jizzum-filled sausage?

It was at the Cave, a polished-up pickup joint in the Glendale Galleria, where Albee Mention, hanging in a club that tried to discourage his presence with the sudden loud strains of country-and-western music the moment he entered, and where he wore his wife, Vera, on his arm and then flashed her so sweetly in their faces, that he introduced Mercy, the white girl du jour, to Doctor Lamont Lester-Allegro.

Strangely enough, Lamont and Mercy hit it off. He found her sweet angel face and her quick sailor mouth anomalous. With hand skills that would make Helen Keller proud, she found nine inches of big-headed, perfectly formed Mandingo meat underneath the table and suddenly he didn't look so square after all.

In a matter of weeks Lamont and Mercy became a clandestine item. Their secret was shared only with Albee and Vera, who relished the deceit perpetrated on Lamont's standoffish, saditty, and ill-cordial wife.

With Mercy the pressure was off. There was nothing Lamont had to prove to himself. Good, bad, or indifferent, he was everything to her. He knew all about her marriage to Joe Jay Randolph and was confident that he, Lamont Lester-Allegro, was the far better man.

He did not always feel the same way about Sadikifu. Still. Not after all these years. And he still could not forget the child Maggie had sacrificed for him. But with Mercy he found a refuge from all those things about himself he did not want to see. Maggie, on the other hand, was the mirror.

He did not know if he loved Mercy as much as he was grateful to her. For that matter, he did not know if he truly loved Maggie. But after so many years of marriage, he had grown accustomed to her, careful with her.

And although he was adventurous with others, he was, still, always careful. He never spent the night away from home, always showered thoroughly when he got up from a bed other than his own, and always carried and put on the same cologne he left home in. He always checked for cum stains. And Maggie was the only one he did not use a condom with.

But over the years Mercy grew impatient with and suspicious of the man she could not have completely. Now, more often than not, their sexual encounters at her Malibu home ended in an ugliness not uncommon to mistresses of someone else's husband.

"Who else are you fucking?"

"What are you talking about?"

"Other than me and your wife, who the hell else are you fucking, Lamont?"

"That's a dumb-ass question, Mercy."

"And that's a dumb-ass answer."

"Look, I gotta get home."

"I'm sick of this shit, Lamont."

"What?"

"It's bad enough I gotta share you with that saditty-ass wife of yours, but now I gotta share you with some other bitch too?"

"I gotta go."

"Well then go! And don't come the fuck back! NIG-GAH!"

And of course Mercy didn't really mean it. Oh she meant the NIGGAH part all right, but the don't-come-the-fuck-back was a lie straight from an aching heart. She had truly fallen in love with Lamont, was addicted to him. All of her privilege—her money, her pussy, and her whiteness—could not afford her the one thing she so desperately needed—to have Lamont Lester-Allegro all to herself.

Months of crying, anonymous phone calls to his house, dog shit on his car handle, stalking, even a serious but ultimately aborted plan to have Maggie killed, preceded the only remedy to her pain. And so, as she stood in his driveway and placed the gun in her mouth, the last thing she thought about was the taste of his dick. Then her nipples stiffened with sudden pleasure, and the blast in her face made her cum.

Chapter Ten

"Just take the goddamn gun, Maggie."

"I don't want the gun, Lamont."

"Look, with all the shit going on out there you better go on and take the goddamn gun, Maggie Arial."

She hemmed and hawed a beat longer, then finally threw her head back with a tad of disdain and tisked . . . and, of course, she took it. After all, in spite of everything, Lamont was right—with all the shit going on out there, "you better go on and take the goddamn gun, Maggie Arial." Gang-bangers cruising Crenshaw Boulevard, drug dealers at fruit stands on Pico and Union, and bad-driver uninsured immigrants every-where—this little two-shot pistol could come in handy some-day. And it did.

But why think about that? Why? Why not think only about how good it was when she was high off Thai stick, liquor, and Luther, and his kisses were warm and familiar—comfortable kisses—sweet, caring kisses; when his touch was gentle and curious, a probing as innocent as a babe and with a knowingness as ancient as forever; when a pastel sun just beyond the terrace was setting, settling in for a good jazz nocturne.

She savored the smell of him and allowed it—the smell of his youth—to dizzy her and weaken her and reduce her to a youthfulness of her own and a foolishness well deserved.

And then she thought about when it got good and nasty. She thought about when gently she ran her fingers through the thick soft naps between his legs and his pretty black dick smiled at her with a swell. Hypnotized by it, mesmerized by it, she found the condom that lay just beneath his propped-up thigh. Without blinking or looking away from the thrill ride, she grabbed it and bit at the edge of its packet, spit out the corner she'd torn with her teeth. Then she struggled to open it; fumbled with it the way she'd fumbled with the joint.

Sparing her dignity, he took it out of her hands.

"You're trembling," he whispered.

"I know," she barely answered. "I didn't think I could again."

She watched hungrily as his throbbing snake stood at full mast while he expertly, artfully, removed the moist shield from the foil. While she bore witness with a shortness of breath she was hard-pressed to survive, he then rolled the vibra-ribbed latex over the thick head of his dick, past the circumcision line, and down the thick veiny shaft with a slow, showy deliberateness. All she could think was that she was the glove, naturally moist, being filled by the boy with the dick of a man.

When finally he entered her, her eyes crossed, her jaw dropped, and her breathing stopped. All of her senses gave holy obeisance to the immeasurable pleasure and damage taking place between her thighs; damage, yes, for after him, she knew, she would never be any good for anyone else.

And so while he fucked her, fucked her good and long, fucked her up and down, softly and roughly, till her head banged against the backboard of his bed and her eyes rolled back and she sucked her teeth, she found herself wondering through all of this good madness just what had she done to deserve all this? What had she done to be in his arms, in his bed, and have him inside her, fucking her like no one had ever fucked her before? Not since Sadikifu had she been fucked with such intense caring and love and supreme satisfaction. All she now knew for sure was that she owed God one. But she would pray her thanks later. For now she would kick back and sweat funky while being ravaged by the touch and the feel of this beautiful child.

It was syncopated lovemaking, always just a little ahead of the fourth beat. It was the kind of slow-churning, pop-smacking lovemaking old blues oracles call "stirring the fudge."

She wanted it to last forever, even though somewhere deep

inside she feared that more of this kind of bliss would kill her. So she cursed him when he finally came and her body trembled again, a series of tiny little tremors, tiny little dances on hot coals that just couldn't help themselves. She felt herself laughing and crying at the same time, her long nails digging into his sweat-streaked torso as it, too, trembled ruthlessly on top of her.

And then she could feel the young boy growing inside her once again, growing to full and satisfying manhood. Tears filled her eyes again as she, with desperation, tried to beg off the intolerable pleasure.

She licked and sucked whorishly at the black nipples on his chest of smoky gold. He whimpered ever so slightly when her licking and sucking became hungry nibbles of that kind of pain one comes to love.

She was carnivorous. She needed meat. And so with a dancer's smoldering obsession and with duty pumped with desire she made him grind her from side to side, up and down, slow and around, while she held on for dear life, held on tightly, fearing and wanting deadly bliss. She held on and cracked the whip, strained the bit, and rode him down until they both collapsed in their newly made puddle of stank.

And then, from out of the sudden still, she, like God looking over the created universe on the seventh day, she, bathing in their sweat, pronounced it "good" . . . "Well done, my son."

He was so much better than the fantasy that had been

building imperceptibly beyond proportion in her mind. All this touching, cloying, fucking evening she silently thanked her lucky stars. She had found a man-child who had blessedly found her center and filled it to overflowing.

Dorian.

Dorian Moore. What more could she have asked for?

She came again, gloriously, fully. And when she did, she cursed him once again, called him "a mighty good mother-fucker!" Then she giggled schoolgirlishly and wondered how a term of such ghetto passion could have escaped her lips, her pristine lips, her saditty, piss-elegant lips. She then let with a deep, graveled vampiresslike chuckle as she lay back just below the square of his chin and deep within dark Hershey's chocolate arms that glistened and reeked of sweet boyhood stench.

Elaine had been oh so right.

"Carry on, Sergeant," Elaine said real nastylike, in a barely audible gutter growl, when she entered the room. She loved watching him torture his body beautiful with weights and barbells. He looked over at her with a casual smile as he continued to pump his iron.

She strutted past him and took in a whiff of his intoxicating odor. On the desk in the corner she placed her briefcase and clicked it open.

"You know, you're really quite a hit."

"Thanks."

"I haven't had a single complaint except from those we can't squeeze in." She searched high and low for her Gucci-covered checkbook. "I could use three more like you. If you run across anyone half as good as you, have them give me a jingle." Ah, there it is, she thought to herself.

"Right."

"Oh, by the way, Senator Maharry?"

"Tuesday, four to six, rush-hour trade."

"She went on for days about last week and the Anton Berg cordials. But just remember, she's back from all that time on retreat—"

"—read: fat farm—"

"—so don't let her do too many of those liquor-filled chocolates. She'll end up gaining back a ton and blaming it on sex."

"No problem."

"Thanks. I can't believe how much I've been running. What with the kids and the parlor and the clients it's been one mad day."

"You should slow down."

"Please. I'm just a poor widow trying to eke out a meager existence. I can't afford to slow down."

"Yeah, right," he smiled wryly without missing a pump.

"Angelus is the only funeral home larger than yours, and that's arguable. You're making big bucks off most of the people that die up here in Baldwin Hills. A poor widow you're not. No. You pimp for the sheer thrill of pimping."

"So why do you whore?"

"Because I'm very good at it. Because you appreciate talent. Because you made me an offer I couldn't refuse."

"And you were smart enough to accept it. Bravo. It's good to see there's more to you than a pretty face and a big dick."

She signed the check and left it on the desk. She turned to him and admired his beauty as he continued to flex. She let out a tiny little sigh, then shook her head with a smile. Only a keen business sense trumped her desire to take him out of her stable and keep him all to herself. He was her best. The money was too good.

"I have someone new for you," she then said. "She's a very good friend. And she's fragile, so make it very sweet."

"What's her name?"

"Maggie. Maggie Lester-Allegro."

"Of *the* Lester-Allegros?

"Yes."

"This should be interesting."

"What's that supposed to mean?"

"When?"

"Tomorrow. Lunch hour at Serenity."

"Got it."

"She'll like you. She needs a lift, some joy in her life, some variety."

"Well, hey, here I am. Designed to fit every mood and depression."

"You know something? You are. You really are. I should give you a raise."

"Yes you should."

"I'll think about it. In the meantime, I have my own particular mood and depression in need of . . . fitting."

"See? There you go again. Hell-bent on eating up the profits."

"That's right, sugah, and in no time at all, I won't have a tooth left in my head."

So he set down his barbells. She put her checkbook aside. He gestured toward the bedroom. She went in before him. And he fucked her in that special way that made her think of Cameron on the j-o-b.

Chapter Eleven

A beautiful baby, he should have been named Onyx. That the adoption was swift was of no surprise to anyone. He was a prize, a golden child. His new parents, Coretta and Malcolm Moore, were devout Jehovah's Witnesses. So he spent his childhood Saturday mornings not in front of cartoons but "spreading the good news of the kingdom through *The Watchtower* and *Awake!* for a small contribution of ten cents."

He was always selling something, if nothing more than a smile.

Everybody at the Kingdom Hall—the entire congregation—called him "mature little Brother Moore" because he always spoke with a comfort and wisdom far beyond his years. His little boy black-as-midnight eyes and his baby dimples and his sweet money smile gave off an old fireplace warmth, and all knew he was blessed when he led them in prayer.

All also knew that he was adopted. Aside from the fact that Coretta and Malcolm were nothing like him in looks, demeanor, and idiosyncrasies, the gift of a child in the Moore household was much ballyhooed throughout every tract home in Del Amo Hills.

And something about the mystery of his parentage gave off perfectly imperfect light and the too sexy angelic little boy engendered the vision of low-hanging fruit to more than a handful—both men and women—at the Kingdom Hall. But no one would dare allow such thoughts of carnal idolatry and sainted debauchery to creep out with sounds greater than a deep inner moan. It was all in the looks. They couldn't look at him without feeling themselves being swept off their feet and in need of catching their breaths and changing their diapers. He had the golden naps of his gorgeous and angry dead father and his real mother's bush queen blue-black beauty.

Mrs. McDaniel—his seventh grade journalism teacher— did what others wanted to do but dared not follow through. She went on and tasted him. She used her new shawl to cushion her knees and save her hose when, one day after school, while they worked late on the yearbook, she sucked his fat little dick behind the paste-up table.

His quiet mystery and beauty caused all to sin in their hearts. Young Dorian Moore was not unaware of this. However, his knowledge was kind and his intentions were never malicious. That too was part of his multifaceted irresistibility: charm, valor, honor, class, discretion, and straightforwardness when called for. He simply went about the business of serving the community in much the same way that he serviced the congregation, with his old fireplace warmth. His black bourgeois clients—secretaries and salesgirls could not afford him—always thought of him to be salvation at a bargain price.

In L.A. terms, the distance between Del Amo Hills and Baldwin Hills was not so great—the 405 North to La Cienega South—but by the time he was only twenty, Dorian had saved enough to lease a place in Baldwin Hills and leave Del Amo, Coretta, Malcolm, and the Kingdom Hall behind him in the South Bay.

And it was within the walls of his new and impeccable cantilevered-view home that he set up shop.

But perhaps "shop" was not the right word. For when the grand and glorious ladies of color came calling it was not like they were shopping. It was more like they were coming to Sunday morning service where the minister prayed over them, for them, and with them. He baptized them and brought them to shouting his name and speaking in tongues. When the collection plate passed in front of them they gladly filled it with weak and breathy thank-yous and went out that day feeling like a champagne brunch at Gaston's.

No. It was nobody's shop. It was a haven. It was heaven. It was Dorian's place.

Serenity was also Dorian's place. It was his office away

from home. The elegant décor, soft amber lighting, and se-
cluded, flowered, and candlelit booths, discreetly accessed
from the Art Deco bar, invited the sort of sophisticated liaisons
Elaine Ramsey and Dorian Moore trafficked in.

And that's where he saw her. What he didn't know could
not hurt him.

Chapter Twelve

One could have only speculated at the depth of Maggie Lester-Allegro's immediate devastation when she realized the terrible truth. One could have only guessed. But the only feelings that had, at the time, touched her mind were feelings of deep caring and being deeply cared for, of loving and being loved. After all, everything costs. And yet, his crying and his warm tears and kitten whimpers while she lay cradled in his arms, sending sweet shivers through her body, should have, perhaps, alerted her to something deeper and sicker, something beneath the surface of this all too perfect May-December business arrangement. But no. Truth would come later. Realization would come later.

Then, Maggie Lester-Allegro was happy being held tightly in his arms. All she knew or needed to remember about that one night almost a year ago to the day was that she had been guided beyond the gates of husband dependency and through the pearly gates of passion and caring by some sweet and lovely young angel that, for some reason, she was never to see again.

And although she parked herself often on her favorite stool at Nuts 'n' Bolts with too many drinks inside her—yet held upright by her great bush dignity and bourgeois sensibility—she knew, for some inexplicable reason, that her vigil was hopeless, that it was only to have been that one night and that she was not to see him again.

If only she could remember the reason why. She had read about it, heard about it, saw it on the news. And now it and he were gone.

It didn't matter—Nuts 'n' Bolts, Serenity, anywhere, nowhere. She was not to see him again; only in her lonely dreams and her smoldering reminiscence melancholied by booze.

It was times like these that made her realize how nice it is to have friends like Elaine, Arleta, and Lydia. These were the kinds of friends whose very existence sang "forget your troubles come on get happy." These were women who did not need men. These were women who knew men, liked men, worked with men, played with men, tolerated them, used them, but need them? No.

It was nice having friends like Elaine, Arleta, and Lydia. It was also maddening. For they did not love men. Maggie believed that from the bottom of her heart.

But she did. She loved men in place of herself. She knew

that now. She gave too much, for she feared she was too little. Was this why Dorian disappeared? Did she chase him away with too much caring, too much dependency? Even as Dorian pleased her and she paid him, she feared that she still owed him. Even as he lay nestled in her arms he needed more. She certainly did.

She did not want that afternoon to end. And in her mind it had not. It was still somewhere up in the air, high above her heart. Infinite. A circle.

Again they made love, then again and again. New positions were tried and new thrills were discovered. She then lay on her back like Juliet on the slab, and she beckoned him over to straddle her face. The sweet, moist, and pungent baby hairs of his tight ass crack met her mouth with a wisp of a kiss. And while his balls, full and fluffy, played round her nose she darted her tongue round the edge of his pucker, teasing his hole till it spasmed and spread. She buried her face deep inside his darkness where she truly found out what true boy pussy was.

Her nose and her tongue and her fingers were in him. He rode her face gently but she wanted more. Her hunger was ravenous and greedy. The harder and deeper she tongue-fucked him the harder his dick got. And the beautiful dick weaved and bobbed with a rocking, and he moaned and groaned with each jab of her tongue. He found himself absently, whorishly, desperately, twisting his nipples. She had conquered his cool but she still was not through. Neither was he. With her tongue deep inside him, he kneeled down between her legs and his tongue found her pussy, and they feasted, perfect sixty-nine rhythm style.

The moans and the slurping, the smacking and spanking went on and on until they both had tears in their eyes. He ate her so ferociously she had to come up for air. And while he worked on her pussy his beautiful ass stared back at her dizzied face with a smile. She grabbed his ass and licked it, then licked balls and sucked dick tucked through thighs taut with pleasure.

She hoisted him up for the best view of it all. She had never seen an ass, balls, and dick so perfectly formed, and for the first time she noticed the two tiny marks on his left inner thigh.

Matching teardrops.

The last thing she remembered was freezing in place and all going blank.

"Remember Dorian Moore?"

"Who?"

"Dorian Moore. Remember? One of my young men on call."

"You mean boy on call."

"You remember him, Maggie."

"She's drunk and she's out of it."

"Let her sleep it off."

"Now who was this again?"

"You remember. Dorian Moore. I saved him for my top drawer clients. The one they found dead about a year ago up on Mount Vernon Drive. Bullet right through that beautiful little birthmark."

"Oh yes. The teardrop murder. I remember him. *The Sentinel* ran a picture on the front page, remember?"

"Right."

"And Gertrude mentioned him in her column."

"That's right, I remember."

"And whoever did it cut his balls off and stuffed them down his throat."

"Oh yes, I remember!"

"What would make you remember a thing like that?"

"I don't know. I was sitting here thinking how fine he was with his pretty young black self, how valuable he was. What a waste."

"What do you mean 'a waste'?"

"What I said, that's what I mean. What a waste."

"You mean a waste of money? What do you mean?"

"I mean a waste of a pretty young black man. As if things aren't bad enough. Pretty young black men are delicacies. That's what they are. A rare and disappearing piece of can't-get-enough satisfaction. Many a dark diva went hungry this past winter. Many were saddened by his untimely and grisly demise. He was one pretty young black man, all the glorious 'else' aside. What a bargain he was. He was better than flowers. I charged a fortune for him, but he was such a steal."

"I am so glad I'm a lesbian."

"I'm so glad you're a lesbian too, baby. Men are too much drama."

"Not as much as the women who crave them."

And as was her drunken custom, Maggie Lester-Allegro sat back silently, listening to Elaine, Lydia, and Arleta go back and forth, back and forth, back and forth, forth and back. And then . . . and then . . . and then it hit her, hit her like a ton of bricks. Her eyes bulged—BULGED!—and her lips stretched wide into some Ross-stricken madness that neither laughed nor cried, just stretched.

Furiously she threw herself away from the table, knocking her chair backward. She stood straight up like a drag queen onstage. With head thrown back and weave shaking in the wind, she screamed and screamed and screamed and screamed and could not stop. Lydia, Arleta, and Elaine looked at her, slowly, as only black Baldwin Hills divas can. And they thought to themselves, separately and together, That's right, girlfriend, let it all out. Ain't nothin' but a song.

It was another perfect day in L.A. The warm afternoon breeze caused the palm trees to shimmy sensually and to rustle with a rhythm. Because the smog had been banished to the open sea, the basin stayed dry, comfortable, and livable. Snowcapped mountains miles in the background posed clear and clean and crisp.

Margaret Arial Lester-Allegro stood out on the balcony of her Baldwin Hills bedroom and took a Baldwin Hills chance. She breathed in deeply. Yes. And it was truly—yes—a chance worth taking. What else would one do in L.A. on a beautiful smog-free day? The air was so clean and so pure. Maggie truly felt as pure and as clean and now cleansed of it all. Everything that needed to be clear was just that. Clear. She couldn't re-member the last time she felt this good. She doubted whether she could ever feel this way again.

She felt herself smiling—the new peace of mind did the trick—and then she puckered her lips, the kind of puckering that widens the eyes without asking a single question. And then she stuck it in her mouth, and while the breeze and the sunshine and the view from the balcony made her feel so good, she still thought of it as all three of them—all of them—in her mouth. Sadikifu. Lamont. Dorian. And while the birds sang in the nearby trees she regretted only the disturbing sound it would make. So she decided not to worry about the sound. She decided not to worry about a damn thang. She was already mellow, and it felt so good . . . so very, very good.

And so she closed her eyes.

And pulled the trigger.

Lamont had tried everything—black women, white women, drag queens—but now he could no longer tolerate any of them: the white woman who killed herself, the black woman who followed suit.

And now, although the house on Don Carlos Drive was all his to do with as he pleased, he did what had pleased him all the years he spent neglecting two women at the same time. He rented their favorite suite at the Century Plaza Hotel and kicked back with his coke and Courvoisier. He lay back on the bed, his blue silk boxers pulled down to his ankles, and stroked himself. He handled himself with a slow rhythmic gentleness while soft-focused videos of their sweet love-making played on and on and on. . . .

And he wondered. Would he? Could he ever get over Dorian Moore?

It's not the world that is my oppressor, because what the world does to you, if the world does it to you long enough and effectively enough, you begin to do to yourself.

—JAMES BALDWIN

Part Two

Chapter Thirteen

"You need to leave them black women alone, Brothaman. They just too stubborn. They want everything their way. They don't know how to appreciate black men."

"Maggie's not like that."

"Then how come you always sneakin' out the house late at night? And don't tell me it's to go get cigarettes. You know, Mercy was crazy for yo' ass. Vera still ain't been able to let it go. So tell me, who you got dyin' over you now?"

Lamont had seen enough drama in the operating room not to lose his cool over this small exposition of this new infidelity. And besides, it was Albee. Only Albee. Someone who would understand the need for such excursions. He could appreciate it. But would Albee understand the concept of him, Lamont Lester-Allegro, yesterday's Negro, with a young man on the side?

The church could not stand it. The silent sissies of the pew would have to call out and 'fess up and tithe extra. His father and a host of Lester-Allegros would be appalled.

"Thank God your mother died in childbirth," Doctor Abner Lester-Allegro would say anytime he was displeased with his son.

But Lamont needed men. He needed pretty young black men who understood the needs of a man from another time who had cheated himself out of the real satisfaction that had awaited him with open arms throughout his youth and young adulthood. He had needs he could not explain. He had unnatural natural needs that manifested themselves only in the closet when lovemaking with his wife was no longer making love or making sense. It had become a duty, a ritual, a blind allegiance to a belief in a family system that could not see the simple concept of love as a God-given gift in spite of the packaging.

"Not that I'm spyin' on you, Brothaman, but you know me. I'm up all hours of the night writin'. I've already done eighty pages on you."

Lamont held the gulp of his extra-dry Tanqueray martini in his throat, not for the sting of the booze, but to not flinch at the sting of his friend's sly and unreadable revelation.

"Don't panic, Brothaman. Hell, it sho' must be good when you gotta keep it a secret from your best friend."

And so in some strange way Lamont Lester-Allegro, having been in a torrid relationship with the sister-in-law of his good friend and neighbor, was assumed to have continued his acceptable clandestine mainstream deceits.

Going out at night continued, even bettered, for now he

could always be considered involved in a perfectly normal heterosexual illicit affair with a white woman while still enjoying the sweet penetration of throbbing young boy meat up an ass with a thirst that never seemed quenched.

Dorian. He thought of him achingly. His mind and heart reeked of him, and it caught him short of breath, long on pain.

Dorian. Lamont had not been quenched of the thirst. Dorian.

Just the thought of young Dorian Moore's sweet-grinding dick stuck so deep up his ass made Lamont whimper a bit, shed a tear, and mourn once again the life he had missed because Daddy had plans of his own.

Daddy. Fuck Daddy.

"You'll grow to love it," Abner Lester-Allegro had said when the opportunity of a marriage between Lamont and Margaret Arial Simpson presented itself. "You'll *have* to love it. Pussy is the Christian thing for a man to love. You know what the Good Book says about that other mess.

"You're a doctor, Lamont. You're good-looking and you're not getting any younger. Most important of all, you're a Lester-Allegro man. That legacy is the only reason people aren't talking yet. Not that I know of, God forbid.

"Hell, son, we've all been out in the field with a little piece of sheep ass, but it's not something that you run around putting on the radio. Marry the girl. And I don't need or want to know about anything else.

"I know, I know. She's a little dark for our taste, especially when you have kids. With you already dark—but that's okay in a man—it might not get you past certain doors, but, hell, things are changing. Dark is beginning to have its say."

And so Lamont, in an effort to be as much of a Lester-Allegro man as possible, married Maggie Simpson, only to discover that his new bride was pregnant with another man's baby. And so he felt like no man at all. Not even the affair with Mercy, a woman who loved the wild thing wild and often and inventive, ultimately did not seem to work for him. She no longer liked the fist upside her head, but a fist inside her pussy, which was just fine with Lamont since, on more than one occasion, he could not command his dick's attention.

And then there was that day, when full of too much cocaine and Courvoisier, he slipped. He told Maggie about the drag queen and the blow job she gave him before he realized she was a he. But he was a cum-too-quick college boy. What did he know? What he didn't tell Maggie was that the drag queen had fucked him like the man he had always wanted to be, fucked him until the walls of his ass were raw. And oh how he loved getting fucked like that. Like he had loved all of those times when being with a man was being alive, only to then hate himself in the too lucid afterglow that always grew stark and accusing.

Daddy. Fuck Daddy.

"Don't forget what happened to Larry Grayson," Abner warned his son.

Daddy. Fuck Daddy.

Dorian Moore. Oh how he missed his Dorian Moore. He remembered well their first encounter: 1988. It was happy hour at Jewel's Room. Lamont had just ordered another double Tanqueray martini. When Marvin the bartender set it down in front of him, he thought he saw an unearthly vision—a beautiful dark vision—in the reflection of the mirror behind the bar. But he held back his startledness when he realized that the only face staring back at him that he even remotely found of sentimental interest was his own face. And what he had thought was an unearthly vision—a beautiful dark vision—was only his want, his fantasy of the pretty young black man he had craved all his life but was too afraid to reach out and touch. It was an untouchable want that flashed brightly in his sad eyes.

But then he was there. Here. From a prayer. A man. A beautiful black-as-midnight man with beautiful black-as-midnight eyes and sparkling white teeth and thick black lashes languid enough and groomed enough to sweep stardust aside. And lips. Lips made full enough to tell a thousand lies.

Lamont sipped softly at his drink and felt warmth deep down inside that place that made him blank to all that surrounded him. He was blank to the music and the madness and the hustlers and the hustled, blank to the vision even as it sat down beside him.

"Hey."

"Hey."

Lamont had to find more breath because breath became short when the beauty sat down. Lamont, being cool, answered "hey" in a register so deep that the bottom end of his vocal cords vibrated deep inside his bowel.

The beautiful boy, with a cordial smile, acknowledged Lamont, who suddenly felt old when the boy turned away toward Marvin the bartender, who knew what was up.

"Cranberry juice," was the call as Marvin nodded and poured him a drink. He was then paid and tipped, and then walked away so nature could take its course.

"You should put something in that," Lamont volunteered out of nowhere, almost shocking himself.

"Like what?"

"I . . . I meant alcohol," Lamont fumbled and blushed.

"Of course you did. What else would you have meant?" asked the pretty young black man with a slyness and gaze that sparkled and burned as he took one more sip. It was a long, sensuous sip. His full lips took to the lip of the glass with a slight smacking. His Adam's apple moved with each swallow. And nervous Lamont was now jealous. Jealous of the glass that the young man tongued. Jealous of the stool that the young man sat on, the pants that held the bulge that widened Lamont's eyes.

The pretty young black man just smiled even more. Lamont, realizing he was staring, pulled out of his trance and turned back to the bar and reburied himself in his double martini. Then the pretty young black man opened up to him.

"My name is Dorian. Dorian Moore"

The introduction caught Lamont off guard. Suddenly the face of his father flashed before him. You're a Lester-Allegro man, Lamont thought quickly, and then responded with a practiced cool, "Lamont Lester."

"Okay, okay, okay. Take Eddie Murphy's ass. You know what can be done to an ass like that? You know what's probably *been* done to an ass like that? I mean, hell, who could resist? Boy pussy of the highest order. That's what he got. He should spend the rest of his life walking bent over and backward. And I bet he got dick for daze too."

A congenial butch queen, who usually frequented the Intermission on Adams near Crenshaw but was making a guest appearance here at Jewel's Room, was holding court at the corner of the bar. Patti LaBelle was screaming from the distant speakers and liquor was in the happy hour revelers that now packed the room.

Lamont and Dorian had much earlier moved from the bar to a table in the corner, away from the ruckus. They drank carefully. Their conversation was the conversation of two men curious, interested, attentive, and hot.

Lamont could hardly believe he was actually sitting with this abstract, unreal person of unreal beauty and infinite attraction, this child-of-God statement.

And then the young man touched his hand. "You're a very handsome man, Lamont."

"Thank you."

"There's something beautifully sad about your eyes."

"Really?"

"Yes."

Dorian slowly leaned over to kiss him. Lamont felt himself leaning in too. Their lips met and brushed and held for a moment, gently. The tip of Dorian's tongue probed Lamont's quivering, parted lips with deferent ease and the beautifully sad eyes closed at the full touch of the kiss. His eyes stayed closed and unmoving, even after Dorian had pulled gently away.

Lamont was lost in a nostalgic trance. He hadn't been kissed like that in years. When finally he opened his eyes, Dorian was smiling at him. Dorian's smile reminded him of Larry Grayson. And Lamont now remembered. Larry Grayson had kissed him that way.

Lamont truly believed he loved beyond the body. Oh the

body was there all right: the face, the smile, the everything physical. But there was a kindness, gentleness, and an attractive softness that was both delicate and masculine in the conversation, questions, and genuine interest that poured forth from the soul of this Dorian Moore.

Lamont had to laugh just a little as his liquor-drenched fantasies redressed him in powdered wigs and stage makeup and happy Hollywood endings. He hardly knew the boy, yet he was already designing their life together, their love together, and their forever together. He had already laid claim to this angel sent to him per his prayer request, although he had not been truly able to put his finger on what it was that he had so desperately prayed for . . . until now.

They had dinner by candlelight at Gaston's and Lamont found himself spilling his guts out in code. As bad as he needed to talk to someone about all of the misery that filled his life, the details were too shameful to put into words. "I don't know how to live," he finally said.

The pretty young black man took his hand. "That's all right, Lamont. I'll teach you."

They checked into a suite at the Century Plaza Hotel. Dorian also lived in Baldwin Hills. Going to his place would not be prudent. On the Hill, little escaped the eyes and ears of Abner Lester-Allegro.

Century City sparkled beneath their window. Linen drapes billowed with a breeze passing through French doors that led to a balcony. Here Dorian schooled Lamont with a roughness that would have made Abner proud. And Lamont took it like a man. The pain made him proud and pleased him greatly. It bolstered him with a newness that could only come from knowing both sides: to give and receive, to have his tight male womanliness filled to the puckered rim, to have his manliness buried in the dark, succulent warmth of good young black booty.

The pretty young black man's pretty fat dick and tight warm behind set off the alarm. And the fire raged on and on, throughout a reminiscence of an affair that could never be repeated.

Lamont awoke with a startle. He was alone. Alone with his coke and Courvoisier. Alone in their favorite suite at the Century Plaza Hotel. Alone in his blue silk boxers. Alone in a life his father had made for him. Alone in his cowardice, his get-along "niggahood." Alone with his memories, his demons, his guilt, his regrets, his wasted life, and the burden he bore over lives he had wasted. Alone with a nature that some found unnatural. He fought hard to escape what was becoming a nightmare. He fought hard to remember only the details of the dream.

And then it hit him. As clear as the new morning sun that now poured through the hotel room window. The last thing he saw before eyes had shot open.

Maggie.

Chapter Fourteen

Ricardo Mathis was one of those black homosexual writers white homosexual publications hire on that rare occasion when something black has to be reported on, acknowledged, answered to, or witnessed.

He was the translator. Bwana's head scout. He broke it down in the King's English, blew on it for those who could not take the heat. He was a West Hollywood snow queen beauty, sought after for expertise on a world he knew little about. But his essays were beautifully written. His short fiction was even better.

Lamont had heard Dorian mention Ricardo before, describe him to a tee. So he knew who he was the moment he walked in on them, saw them together on the floor of the sunken living room.

Dorian had warned Lamont many times before: "Don't fall in love with me." But Lamont could not help it.

"Your eyes are too sad."

"You used to think they were beautiful."

"They once were. They were beautifully sad. Now they're just . . . sad."

Lamont, more obsessed than he realized, braved the threat of community exposure and went to Dorian's house on that fateful night. He parked around the corner, entered through Dorian's side gate, then with a surgeon's precision, jimmied Dorian's back door. He came through the kitchen toward the soft light and the sound of Luther crooning romance. And there they were, locked in a blue-light sixty-nine.

Lamont froze and could not look away. And even as their eyes—all four of them—seemed to rise up to see him at the same time, the sucking and cheek bulging, the ball licking and salad tossing, did not decrease. The shock of his presence paled against the inertia of good foreplay destined to be out-done by great sex to come. Ricardo had been with so many white boys who worshiped him with begging cries of "Fuck me! Fuck me, you black motherfucker! Fuck me with that big black dick!" that the very thought of him now being the white boy butt-fucked by a black buck made his titties swell and his dick drip like Karo syrup. Whenever he was with Dorian he was Miss Ann in the hand of a half man/half beast that could have easily been his physical twin and still his soul's foe.

And now the other twin stood in the door: the sad-eyed twin with murder in his sad eyes. But Ricardo paid Lamont lit-tle mind—did not care who he was or why he was there.

Ricardo simply continued to suck on the dick that would fuck him so dearly, while making a quick mental note: a perfect short story for *Advocate Men*.

Dorian lifted himself up from Ricardo's pubic nest and leaned back, enjoying the blow job with a gracious cool. He looked over at Lamont once again. But Lamont was gone. Dorian felt a relief that was as good as the head he was getting. Lamont could not understand, would not understand, that Dorian had something for everyone, that Dorian was a generous soul who always had to be in the position to serve where the need was great, or merely desired. Lamont could not understand that. But now he had seen with his own beautiful sad eyes.

Dorian pulled his dick out of Ricardo's mouth with a pop and a teasing. Ricardo strained for the dick with the tip of his tongue. He whimpered as he was allowed one last lick at the jizzumy slit. Dorian then turned Ricardo over, rolled on one of the black ribbed condoms Ricardo always brought with him, and gave him the doggy-style fucking he came across town from West Hollywood to get.

Lamont watched from the window and cried.

The view of the city from his bedroom window so sparkled below that it seemed religious. The light lining the basin was a neon swirl of pastel fluorescence. The stars above shimmered against the clear black lid of the sky like tiny scattered diamonds.

Lamont saw none of this. Demons distracted him. He tossed and turned in his bed, deep in a tumultuous sleep filled with the mockery of the dead and the condemnation of the living. They sashayed in front of him, fucked snow queens before him, delighted in his motherless childhood, had babies that weren't his, and demanded from him what seemingly could not be.

"The least you could do is give me a goddamn grandchild that lives," the echoed voice demanded.

Many a night they dropped by to see him, to haunt him, to haze him, to remind him. Slowly but surely, the reminders began to take their toll. And a pretty young black man would end up dead.

Lamont knew he would never have the strength or the nerve or the courage or the guts to do what Maggie had done, to do what Mercy had done. He would die a natural death that would come after such an unnatural life.

His grief and despair were borne of cowardice. He was cloaked in deception created by guilt, shame, and self-loathing. He knew these things about himself and the knowing made him hate himself more. So when a rescuer appears and holds out a hand, then snatches it back, that instigator of so cruel a prank must die. Lamont was just one of many pathetic souls in the world who needed to be spared the cruelty of snickering angels.

How many more had fallen in love with Dorian only to be rebuked by him? Why would salvation spit in your face when you're flat on your back?

He believed Dorian had to die and that he, Lamont, had to do the killing. He had to get rid of the pretty young black man to save himself, redeem what little was left of himself.

Lamont had killed a pretty young black boy before; the one once inside him. And when that boy was aborted and shitted out Lamont felt the relief that comes with that kind of emptiness.

During those few precious times he shared with Dorian he was almost feeling all right, almost believing that the way that he was was all right.

"It's all right, Lamont Lester," love spoke and he knew it, "but don't fall in love with me."

"How could I not?"

"Don't do that to me. Don't do that to you."

But the taste of the boy was dope through the schoolyard fence. Lamont was hopelessly addicted after just one hit: a junkie punk bitch hooked, lined, and suckered.

He hated himself all over again, hated himself for loving what should not be loved.

He thought he had been flushed clean of that part of himself, but Dorian Moore was the painful reminder. So Dorian Moore had to die.

But the death of the boy exorcised nothing. When Dorian was found with his balls in his mouth Lamont felt no release. He went mad, truly mad, vexed by the passion-filled crime he was convinced he'd committed.

His demons dragged him through the streets screaming confessions of murder. He confessed to anyone within earshot, to the high heavens, in a mad and feverish way that disturbed the conservative calm of his neighbors. But his confession provided no solace, no pathway to light.

He then took to dancing naked and angry, first in the living room, then poolside, then out on the sidewalk in front of his house, pissing down his leg while sprinklers baptized him. He howled at the sky, "I did it! I had to! I killed him! God made me!"

Elois Andrews from across the street was the first to respond to the raucous ranting. On one particularly memorable day her mouth dropped at the sight of him. She stood frozen in place until Francine Harvey next door poked her head out and Lawd-have-mercy'ed herself into head shakes and foot pats.

"I cut off his balls! I stuffed them down his throat!"

Others had gathered but all were afraid to approach the wild dog. Finally Albee Mention ran out of his house with a blanket. He covered his friend and was fought for his efforts. But Albee would not give up. He held Lamont tightly until Lamont could fight no more. Lamont collapsed in Albee's arms and cried like a baby and sucked on his thumb.

Someone had called the police, discreetly of course. When they arrived they retrieved him from Albee with deference. He was still a Lester-Allegro. They'd been told that on dispatch.

He wailed and fought them and begged them to kill him. When they politely took him away, neighbors gathered and gossiped in hushed tones about all the years of Lester-Allegro high drama on Don Carlos Drive: the stillborn baby, the white woman dead in the driveway, the wife's suicide on the balcony. And now this. Baldwin Hills was becoming as bad as the foothills, known as "the Jungle."

"I did it! I had to! I killed him! God made me!" he cried to his jailers. But no evidence could be found to support his claims. Out of respect for Doctor Abner Lester-Allegro's power, the details of the false arrest brought on by a false confession do not exist in the files of Los Angeles County. So back to the streets Lamont remanded his case. Naked and nasty, with hair matted and nails caked with feces and dirt, he continued his tirade until his father could stand it no more.

Abner Lester-Allegro, with regret and relief, had his son discreetly locked up in an asylum by the sea. And there Lamont Lester-Allegro stayed—mumbling, mumbling, mumbling—while the voice of his wife sang love songs by Luther with hidden meanings and visions of pretty young black men danced gently in his jingle-jangle mind.

Chapter Fifteen

I n time, calm would return to Baldwin Hills. The big Northridge earthquake, the Rodney King beating, O.J. and the verdict-induced uprising blessedly distracted from a community ill-desirous of scandal and spotlight. The Lamont Lester-Allegro situation was but a blip on black bourgeois L.A.'s radar screen now, and they were fine with that. Mayor Tom Bradley was a god in this city and Councilman Abner Lester-Allegro was the mayor's archangel.

County Supervisor Yvonne Braithwaite Burke controlled the purse strings of L.A. County, the eighth largest economy in the world. The glut of black multimillionaire actors, singers, showbiz executives, and athletes who quietly used their fortunes to buy influence and build an economic nation headquartered here in the City of Angels was no aberration. The preservation of that black influence in a city where blacks only represented 12 percent of the population was no joke. More rich black people lived in Los Angeles than in any other major city in the United States. And L.A. black folk—adjustable, tolerant, smarter than they ever let on to be, and blind when the sun shines too harshly—were not about to have their clout eroded by something as insignificant as suicide, homosexuality, murder, and insanity. The sins of the son would not be visited upon the father or the community. Social patricide would not be tolerated by the city's black elite.

Lamont Lester-Allegro was declared re-sane by 1999. When the healed and handsome fifty-three-year-old was released into the care of his now ancient father (in his fifth term as the District 8 councilman, recently and barely defeating his strongest challenger to date, the popular tough-on-crime and openly lesbian jurist, Lydia Titus), Baldwin Hills acted as if he'd only been on sabbatical.

"You see, that's the difference between you and Lydia Titus, Dad. When she sees a rat she sees a rat. When you see a rat you see a meal."

Lamont's father just knew that his son could never say something like that to his face, not his face, not deliberately, not his son. Tourette's syndrome. Yes, that's it, because his son—not to his face, not from his son—would never. EVER!!! And besides, he had to remember. His son, the sole heir to his standing, his place, his smudge on the forehead of the anointed, had just gotten out of a facility sensitive to sensitives and would need that tender loving care that would bring him into his destiny in the scheme of family things.

Abner Lester-Allegro was up there in age. So was his

younger brother, Gregory. It was a sad fact that both these aging nobles seemed to produce nothing but offspring who grew up to be little more than burdens and embarrassments. It seemed that the Lester-Allegros, much to their practiced astonishment, could not maintain legacy no more than they could beat out mortality.

For all intents and purposes, Lamont and his two cousins, Will and Champion, were the last of the Lester-Allegros. The three of them were childless in one way or another. Lamont had fathered no children physically. Will's only child, pissed by family and peer pressure to marry and procreate, abandoned the family's traditional AME faith for Catholicism, joined the priesthood, and dedicated himself to a life of celibacy.

Champion's oldest was shot in a drive-by during a Compton crack buy gone wrong. His younger, hating his family for everything it pretended to be, had himself fixed so he would never bring another fucked-up Lester-Allegro into this world. Will and Champion Lester-Allegro, disappointed by their offspring and disappointing their ancestors, followed each other into early graves. Lester-Allegros were piling up like dead Kennedys.

So although a minor hope, Lamont was the only hope—not yet dead and the only one left to bet the family beads on. Thank God his treatment was effective.

After years of incarceration, he attained acceptable lucidity. He was reborn and experiencing his childhood again, this time in an unencumbered, un-Lester-Allegro way. The Meadowbrook Rest Home-by-the-Sea was like a mother's womb, giving him a floating protection while he developed his vital parts: a brain, heart, mind, and body. Perhaps even a soul.

But it was indeed a long and painful process. He was forced to face things about himself, about his family, about his nature, burdens, and blessings.

The first few weeks at Meadowbrook were the hardest. Lamont howled, kicked,. and cursed relentlessly, threw himself against walls, forcing staff to bind him down for his own safety's sake. On those nights when his fits exhausted him into sleep or medication was resorted to, his dreams became nightmares, indictments for being born and living lies. He cried every day of those first few weeks. His doctor allowed him to, waited patiently to glean from his wailings psychological morsels that could hint at the problems, give clues to solutions.

"When she comes to you in your dreams, what does she say?" the doctor asked one day.

"Why?" Lamont answered in between wails. "She keeps asking, 'Why?' "

"And the young man you thought that you murdered . . ."

"Did murder! Did murder!"

"When your wife comes to you, why do you think she asks 'why?' What is she asking?"

"Why was I born?" he cried, "Why did I marry her? If we

couldn't love each other, why couldn't we at least love our-
selves?"

"Why were you born?" the doctor then asked.

"Because somebody came."

"Why did you marry her?"

"I did it for God. I didn't want to burn in hell."

Lamont had never wanted to be a doctor. That was his father's
desire. At the age of thirteen Lamont Lester-Allegro only
wanted two things in his life: wings and Larry Grayson.

It was the late summer of 1959 when the Graysons took
over the house across the street. The Berringers, a congenial
enough white family of four, had seen the changing tide in
Baldwin Hills, where white flight emptied out the grand
abodes that overlooked the city from poolside terraces. Newly
rich Negroes and entertainers like Ike and Tina Turner, Nancy
Wilson, and Ray Charles were now claiming the castle views.
The Berringer family was one of the few holdouts who indeed not only got along well with their new Negro neighbors
but also actively socialized with them. They entertained one
another in one another's homes. Christmas, birthday, and an-
niversary gifts were exchanged. Funerals were attended mutu-
ally. Their children alternated sleep-overs.

But in what had been a subtle reversal of certain cove-
nants, the community council, led by Dr. Abner Lester-

Allegro, had made the Berringers a financial offer that could not be refused. The neighborhood could now be transformed into a true black bourgeois enclave of discriminating taste and selective values. The black bourgeois Graysons were chosen to buy.

In his room, caped in bedsheets, thirteen-year-old Lamont bounced on his down-feather bed, determined to reach the ceiling while determining the age of the boy across the street, who himself was watching diligent moving men move museum-grade paintings and high-back chairs and a baby grand piano and fringed Persian rugs from truck to house.

And then later that day, when the sun chose to set in its own tangerine, music poured out from the Grayson house. Music. Piano. Classical. Impressionistic. Ravel. *Claire de Lune.* Soft. Delicate. Quiet. Hypnotic. Passion. Falling feathers. The sound. And he knew. It drew him across the street, drew him closer. He found himself without knowing it moving up the long, ascending staircase. And from nowhere he was at the door where the soft and gentle music would not allow him to bat an eye. He raised a hand and slowly balled it, but could not knock. The soft and gentle music would not allow it.

He found himself moving, floating, to the window, the large and sparkling picture window that had not yet been draped, although the drape he wore, the cape to fly, he did not even realize he was still wearing. All he knew was the music was the boy: the beautiful, beautiful boy, sitting at the piano, caressing the keys with gentle fingers.

His own gentle fingers that had been balled to knock were now spreading wide open like sunflowers bathing in sunshine. Both his hands, soft and begging, moved up the glass to frame the face that was a hairsbreadth away from the wall that separated them.

He stared long at him with those unbatting eyes, the eyes of the child that he was. His sweet aching was so softly electric, that the boy—the piano player—was drawn to look up toward the light beaming toward him.

As their eyes met, music continued, fingers played on, open hands climbed the window, and baby's breath fogged the glass.

The piano player smiled. And Lamont saw the dimples . . . the dimples . . .

They became puppy-lovers and friends, involved in a sweet mist borne from a similar urge and nature. What they did, what they felt, what they dreamed were the doings, feelings, and dreams of young boys in love, unfettered by the ills that hovered just above their heads.

And so when Mr. Grayson found them naked and kissing playfully, intently, earnestly, uniquely perverted, he could do nothing but stare at first. He was stunned into silence. Then from a small distance the even tone voice of reason called out without any indications: "Lawrence."

And Lawrence Grayson climbed down off Lamont Lester-Allegro and pulled his pants up over his stiff little dick. His father walked over to him, looked at his face, then down at his dick, then down at the other boy, whose naked and shivering ass pointed toward the sky.

"You. Get out. I don't want to ever see you near my son again. Understand me?"

Tears that streamed down Lamont's face were shared with shame and sorrow.

He ran from the room, through the halls, toward the door, down the driveway, across the street, into the house, toward the parlor, into the arms of Mrs. Jackson, the housekeeper. And the phone was ringing before Mrs. Jackson had a chance to ask him what was wrong. He couldn't have answered her anyway.

His crying was the hiccuped kind that snatched at every word attempted, staccato wailings washed in eye water.

Doctor Abner Lester-Allegro answered the phone while Mrs. Jackson asked the crying boy kindly, "What's wrong, baby? What's wrong?" And then suddenly little Lamont could hear only his crying. The ringing had stopped. The muffled sound of his father on the phone had stopped. Abner's stone-cold expression caused Mrs. Jackson to stop. The world had stopped while Lamont's tears lived on.

In a moment he caught himself. He sucked the last tear back with a baby's pity. He looked up and his father was standing before him, looking at him with eyes that burned with righteous indignation and dignified disgust.

"Mrs. Jackson, excuse us please," Abner said to his employee without taking his eyes off his shivering son. Mrs. Jackson said "Yes sir" to her boss's back as he led his son out of the kitchen.

Up the winding staircase he escorted the boy as if to an execution.

Lamont sat on the bed in his room. His father surveyed the space he rarely entered. He stood over his son with hands firmly behind him, feet planted Pershing-like, eyes burning down. Lamont could not look up. His eyes counted the swirls and the pegs of the mahogany floor.

"I can't say that I'm surprised," Abner Lester-Allegro finally said. He then stared at the framed picture of Lamont's dead mother hanging over the bed. "Your mother always wanted a little girl. I guess that's what she got, God rest her soul." He then went to the window and stared down at the house of the new neighbors. Containment would be the order of the day. "I knew it from the beginning." He continued to stare out the window, his eyes now keen to the sky that blessed and cursed, but recognized him. "You cried all the time, like a little girl. Like a little bitch. If I thought I could beat it out of you, I would have, but the stain has set too long.

"Nevertheless, you are my son. You are my child. Most important, you're a Lester-Allegro and you will not disgrace me beyond this perverted nature of yours." Abner moved away from the window and perused the room, looking for telltale signs, hints he dreaded finding but was brave enough to face and correct.

"You will not think about boys in that way ever again. You will remove that from your heart. And if you don't, God will snatch out your heart and feed it to the fires of hell." And for the first time in his son's room, he looked down at his son, forcing Lamont to look up at him. "I may not know what you're thinking. But God will. He will be watching you and listening to you and knowing what you feel. You will not be able to hide it from Him. So cleanse your thoughts right here and right now. Or God will come for you and burn your sinful heart in hell."

And every day after that Lamont Lester-Allegro feared God's knock at his door. But as much as he tried, he could not get Larry Grayson out of his mind.

Within the month the brakes on the Graysons' car failed and the car rolled down the driveway, striking Larry, killing him instantly while he fixed his bike. Lamont wailed and beat the ground with his fists and threw himself against the wall until he broke his arm. Then and there he knew that God had come for him, had come to burn his sinful heart in hell.

The doctor did not say a word. He sat there while Lamont cried. Telling the story was telling. After so many years, speaking the words for the very first time was a healing. The pain was the pain of good surgery. After ten minutes of cleansing boohooing, Lamont felt drained and flushed out, an exhaustion that comes with a vigorous workout, and he could not explain the calm. The doctor was not about to explain it to him.

They met weekly, the doctor and Lamont. Each meeting had less and less crying, more and more stories of fathers and sons who had neither wives or mothers to run to, to be sheltered by, to be told "It's all right, baby;" fathers and sons who had crippled themselves in the absence of nurturing.

Each subsequent meeting became less "woe is me" and simply asked "Why?" like Maggie's first question. And the answer eased up: eventual, patient, not checking the clock, finally.

Because that is how God made me. And Abner Lester-Allegro is not God.

Over the years by the sea, Lamont was visited less and less by his wife singing Luther. He had come to see the "himself" he thought he had murdered so long ago. The face of Dorian had become his face. He felt compassion for that little boy that he now knew was him. Hints of the reasons and therefores began to appear from the haze, imperceptive still, but more promising then ever before.

He was ready to go when they let him go. And yes, he would take control of the family business. The Lester-Allegro Group would continue to prosper under the reign of the newly sane son.

Chapter Sixteen

"Well I'll be," Elaine said when she saw him in the Baldwin Hills mall. Her smile was a glance back at history. "Lamont Lester-Allegro. I thought that was you."

Now sixty, she was still beautiful in her own indelible way. Her tasteful, nonapologetic makeup didn't hide what—on a less self-assured woman—would be considered a plain-Jane face of undistinguished features. She was still the hot black lady; she was still the real Miss Thing.

"Elaine," he said with a casual smile.

"I heard you were back."

"Yes I am . . ."

". . . And looking as good as ever." She looked him up and down. She had not lied. "How was life on the continent?"

"You mean Santa Barbara."

"Santa Barbara? But I thought . . . I mean, your father said you were . . ."

"Dad's been known to confuse things."

"All this time, I'm thinking you're in Africa, up to your chin in tropical medicines. I just knew you'd be the first to come up with an AIDS cure or something, prizes and things."

"Unfortunately not."

"All this time, you've been right upstate."

"Yep."

"And not a word."

"Yep."

"How about a drink?"

"Sure."

"Serenity?"

"Fine."

Serenity had changed very little in the many years that had passed since Elaine made deals for those in search of fun, relief, and/or comfort. All that was behind her now. The death of Dorian Moore took the fun away.

But Lamont's presence rekindled the memory of a time and the memory of a service. Seeing Lamont again made her think back to the early days, before Maggie, when she could've had a Lester-Allegro in her stable. What a coup that would have been. She could have made a fortune off him: a hot young bourgeois black beauty, home for the summer from his Ivy League college, selling good high-class dick to a finicky clientele. If only he had been willing.

But what had been missed was gone for good. Still, she

marveled at how fine and refined he still was, after all he'd been through.

And no. Elaine Ramsey did not have to probe beyond the hushed rumors. Lamont had already cosigned them. He had not been in Africa all those years—he said so himself—but had indeed been hospitalized for a severe nervous breakdown shortly after Maggie's death. Everybody in the know, which was a very small circle, knew where he was and, out of respect for Doctor Abner, went along with the dignified tale officially told.

"How long has it been, Lamont?"

"Ten years. Twelve. I lose count." He was so much mellower than she would have expected. "You look great," he continued, startling her. "Still."

"I guess," she purred, unable to keep herself from eyeing his fifty-three-year-old bulge. "The kids are all grown and married with kids. Their kids have kids. I'm a great-grandmother now."

"You were always great at everything."

"True."

"I wish I'd been a better husband. I wish I hadn't been a husband at all. That would have been so much better for the both of us."

"Now, now. That's all water under the bridge. You both suffered through some unbelievable times and situations. We all did."

"Not you. You never suffered. You only made bucks."

"From bringing others pleasure? I could think of a lot worse vocations."

"Bringing the world carnal pleasure has always been your thing, hasn't it?"

"My, my. Extended vacations have made you judgmental. Did you find God? Are you saved now?"

"Saved from what?"

He was cool-snapping, going off in an offhanded way, reading in a lower register. The game was in play.

"You never liked me much, did you, Lamont?"

"I don't know if I've ever given it much thought."

"You thought about it once."

"Did I?"

"How quickly they forget . . . or choose to."

"Oh yes. Now I remember. Before the Ice Age. When I was a spring chicken."

"And now you're just chicken.

No, baby. I'm all beef. Finally."

Then out of nowhere Lamont snapped his fingers and Elaine didn't get it. With everything on TV, in the news, on the streets, in the churches, she was clueless, still, at sixty.

"You never understood did you?" he then said.

"Understood what?" Her reply was rhetorical.

"That I never wanted you."

"Never?" She preened incredulously.

"When I was seventeen, I was just a boy. And what we had was just plain sex."

"Oh yes," she purred, with it all coming wonderfully back to her. "You were just another pretty young black thing: young, dumb, and full of cum, looking to get your newly filled rocks off. It's a shame you never needed me."

"Maggie needed you, Elaine. Not me. I never needed to pay for it. I never needed to get paid for it."

"What ever do you mean?"

"I only hope that you treated her well."

"So all this time, you knew."

"You and Maggie were very close friends. You don't pal around with a pimp without trying out the samples."

There was that snap again.

"Excuse me?"

"Yes, I knew you procured for her. I knew it as well as you know I wasn't away in Africa."

"Santa Barbara, you said."

"Santa Barbara is a great place."

"It only happened once, you know."

"What only happened once?"

"Finding Maggie pleasure."

"Don't be silly, Elaine. Maggie liked you like a sister. You gave her pleasure often."

"You know what I mean. The boy trade. It only happened once."

"Sometime once is all it takes. She seemed happy after that, for a brief moment, and I was happy for her."

"Yes, I believe she was."

"I don't think I ever found it, though it certainly wasn't for not looking."

"Oh yes. Albee's sister-in-law."

"Who?"

"Has it been that long?"

"Mercy . . . oh yes."

"Was that her name?"

"Yes . . . the things I've done. The things I'll never do again."

"Boy, was that a mess."

"You don't know the half of it."

"So tell me something, Lamont. In all those years, did you ever learn to love?"

"I'm still working on it. . . . If I had it to do all over again . . ."

"You'd do absolutely exactly what you've done."

"No I wouldn't."

"Yes you would. You're a Lester-Allegro."

"Not anymore."

"You know, that's all she really wanted."

"To be happy?"

"Yes."

"And to be loved."

"Oh yes."

"So do I, Elaine . . . so do I . . ."

"Hey lookahere Brothaman I have to write what I'm feeling and if what I'm writing is too much for them to digest well then maybe they need to find something more suitable to they digestive system like chicken see 'cause I write chittlin' and a lot of people don't like chittlin' and that's okay 'cause for the people that like chittlin' they read my shit stand up and slap they mamma but for the otha ones fuck 'em and feed 'em chicken."

They were high again. Like old hippies in headbands and love beads, they sat on the floor before the fireplace, passing the joint back and forth, back and forth, forth and back, in slow motion, contemplating the mellow majesty of each swerving flame. The crackle that formed a symphony was just the kind of music they wanted to hear, so they sat silently, reverentially, hushed, sometimes frozen in midpass, while the embers sang before a stack of neatly rolled joints and a small hill of good coke heaped neatly on the glossy cover of Albee Mention's thirteenth bestseller.

"Guess who I ran into the other day?"

"Who?"

"Elaine Ramsey."

"She still got her homes?"

"Yep."

"Was nothin' ever dumb about Elaine Ramsey."

"Yep."

"She still pimpin'?"

"Who knows?"

If Lamont's eyes weren't so heavy with the high they would have sparkled at the observation, but instead, they sat as lazy as his lips, lips that only emitted a smiling "humph." Lamont hadn't smoked a joint or done coke in years, so when invited over by his longtime friend, he hit and snorted a few times, just a few. Just enough to glaze his eyes over and soothe him into a thing that made him think of love. And this time as he thought of it, it did not sadden him. In fact, it was this that made his lazy lips laugh, his lazy eyes sparkle, and his lazy heart beat.

So do I . . . so do I . . .

He heard himself say the words. He saw himself sitting there, across from Elaine, his dead wife's best friend. He heard himself say what his wife must have said perhaps a thousand times. That's what she wanted, that's what they talked about. The happiness. And he too wanted the same—perhaps wanted it so strongly that it blinded him to the wants and the needs of a woman whose life he had most assuredly destroyed. Love, happiness, forgiveness. That's what he wanted.

Chapter Seventeen

She woke many a night from dreams of her long-since-dead undertaker feasting between her legs, only to discover that fingers were all that she had. But the dream was there. All the years. All the times. And it was almost as good as the man. If she could only remember . . . only remember.

Oh, she had a boy or two that she sugamammied every now and then. Young USC types from South Central with big black obedient dicks and plenty of time to ride an old girl around the track field. But there was no one like Dorian Moore to take her melancholied mind off Cameron on the j-o-b. And there was no one like Cameron to show her what life and love really meant.

But they were dreams. Dreams. Not nightmares, no bad mind games, no tearful reminiscences. Merely dreams.

How old was she then, when he swept her off her feet and made her his queen? Cameron. A man who never crossed a giving heart.

Spread the love. Spread the joy. That's what she learned. That's what he taught her. That's what he gave.

Love . . . and happiness. And pretty young black men would be the vessels. That's what she knew.

He had died doing what he loved: giving her head to the point of a nosebleed. It was too much for his heart. But there was a smacking smile frozen on his face and a stiff penis dripping in his hand, neither one easily prodded from the erotic tableau.

And so she moistened herself and played with her titties and moaned at the thought of him eating her out while sweet Dorian pounded her ass from behind.

Cameron was her last great fuck of the century. Dorian was the reminder. A reminder of what she would not have again. She loved sex as much as she loved love. She had no shame in her claim. And as she served Dorian up to the grateful sistahs of society, she truly wanted to keep him for herself. He was the newborn ghost of Cameron past. He was the sweet, young reminder that there was still joy in the world, pleasure to be had, children who give comfort.

She wanted him for herself, yet knew his gift was just that. A gift. Not her personal treasure to be hidden away in some dark vault and brought out on that rare occasion when special drag and special jewels are called for.

But she could not help her hungry self. She wanted him. Stingily. Jealously. So each time she paid him his commission, she pinched off a little of him for herself. She got hers. Hers, so that she would not feel left out, forlorn, double-widowed with nothing to look forward to. So that she would not be driven to murder, to the killing of the golden goose, to the none-for-all that truly and sadly came to pass. And when he died she tried her best to play it off, to make believe that losing him was loss of business only. She had to believe that. She had to pretend to, for she was on the brink of confession, until she heard that Lamont had taken the blame, had thought that *he* had killed the boy who pleased the wife that he himself could not make happy.

And so out of quiet gratitude and knowing tea only the discreet could sip, she introduced Lamont to the man whose beard and dreads were red and gold with gentle streaks of gray. And the man smiled. And Lamont smiled back, taking the outstretched hand firmly into his.

"Lamont Lester-Allegro."

"Raymond Harris Sr."

"My pleasure."

"Elaine tells me you used to be a doctor."

"A long time ago. I'm involved in the family business nowadays."

"Right. The Lester-Allegro Group."

"So what line are *you* in?"

"I write for the *Times*."

"Features? Editorials?"

"Obits. That's how I met Elaine. I did the copy on Raymond St. Jacques and Esther Rolle."

"Really?"

"It's an art."

"Well, I would think. After all, it's writing."

"Celebration in light of sadness."

"Exactly."

"Completely dichotomous."

"Totally."

"Isn't that the new county supervisor?"

"Lydia Titus. Yes."

"Thought so. It's a new world, isn't it?"

"Yes it is."

"Jackie Goldberg, Lydia Titus, *Will & Grace*, *Queer Eye*, gay marriages just around the corner. I guess Pat Robertson, Bishop Blake, and all the other dinosaurs better go find a rock to die under."

"Lydia Titus and my late wife were very good friends."

"I'm so sorry, I mean, about your wife."

"Thank you. It was a long time ago."

"Wait a minute. Lamont Lester-Allegro. Margaret Arial Lester-Allegro?"

"Yes."

"I wrote the obituary."

"Did you?"

"I hope you were pleased."

"From what I remember, I was very pleased."

Elaine was back from making her third hostess round. "Did Raymond tell you he used to be a Black Panther?"

"Really? And you have a son."

"How did you know?"

"The 'senior' part. Elaine introduced you as Raymond Harris Sr."

"Oh yeah, that's right. He died a long time ago."

"I'm sorry to hear that."

"It was a long time ago. He died in the movement. The late sixties. A long time ago."

"I'm sorry . . ."

"Yeah."

But Lamont Lester-Allegro could clearly see that to Raymond Harris Sr. the loss of his son way back in the 1960s seemed like a loss as near as yesterday, the gash still bleeding, and the pain still there. Lamont knew easily that this man carried the "senior" as part of his name to keep the memory of a martyred son ("he died in the movement") in its loving place of honor and affection.

"Fathers should die before their sons."

There had been a long silence. An uncomfortable one, where the hum of the party around them, lulled by the soft jazz of the tuxedoed trio at Elaine's baby grand, wailed out the unspoken.

"Fathers should die before their sons."

That's all he said within the silence. And Lamont felt ashamed for understanding all too well.

"Elaine really knows how to throw a party."

"Yes she does. Isn't that the mayor?"

"Yes it is."

"Well, one thing about ol' Elaine, she'll cross party lines in a minute for a good cast."

"Same ol' Elaine."

"Yeah, same ol' Elaine."

Lamont did not know what it was about Raymond Harris Sr. that kept him in this conversation most of the night. But there was something. Something familiar yet foreign. A comfortable brotherhood that he could only guess at as his past offered no experience in recognizing the condition. Also Raymond Harris Sr. was older than Lamont. Maybe fifteen years older. He seemed the kind of father type Lamont would have wanted. They shared similar pains, similar losses, and perhaps similar sins.

"My wife talks to me at times," Lamont found himself saying. "She comes to me at night. She calls my name. She says it softly. And every time I try to explain, she says, 'Shhhhh.' And I do. And I feel . . . I feel . . ."

But Lamont could not describe what it was that he felt, but he suspected that what he felt was what Raymond Harris Sr. felt. And that was what they shared. Without saying it, without knowing it, they were bound in some inexplicable way to the losses that they imagined as such senseless, mindlessly masterminded losses.

And so from the grave two spoke—a father's son, a husband's wife—to two who still suffered life, filled with guilt's pain.

"Look at us. You a former Panther, me an ex-doctor; I guess we both gave up on trying to save the world."

"I guess we did, didn't we?" Raymond said softly. The party that buzzed around him no longer mattered. The surroundings were just a blur except for Lamont Lester-Allegro's words: *I guess we both gave up on trying to save the world.*

How ironic, Raymond mused with a sadness he did not like to reveal. He was reminded again that he wasn't even able to save his son.

Chapter Eighteen

Raymond Harris Jr. died the way Raymond Harris Sr. would have, had the opportunity presented itself. To have been able to take the place of his son in death would have made death the soothing alternative to the living, guilt-ridden hell he was left to exist in. But it was the son who was taken, a death prompted by insidious times and the fury of a father unwilling to take society's abuse anymore.

Reared by an anger induced by a city that gave black people hell, Raymond Harris Jr., by the time he was fifteen in 1965, was as sick of the oppression as his father was at thirty-five. The father-son anger that year was energized by Malcolm's revelations of devils in white sheets seen and unseen. Men burning with the fire of enough-is-enough, Malcolm-articulated black rage and black pride all came to a head in the heat of that summer and a fuse ignited, its atomic fallout still felt to this day.

While Raymond Harris Sr. stood up to police that started off calling him "boy" and ended up beating his ass, Raymond

Harris Jr. learned. While Raymond Harris Sr. was losing a wife who wanted only to make love, not war ("You high yellow niggahs always got to be the blackest"), Raymond Harris Jr. was learning. The marches, protests, and civil unrest that flared in the summer of 1965 cosigned everything his father taught him. But the father, years later, now doubted commitment to a war in which his own child would be laid dead on the battlefield.

Raymond Harris Sr. became Omoro, a Black Panther faithful. His son became Sadikifu Omoro. And while Aretha sang for "Respect," black people in America weren't getting any. The time had come to not only demand but also take what was rightfully owed. The Watts Riots of 1965 lit the keg.

By 1968 the mule that came with the forty acres of crumbs was kicking society in the head with a vengeance. The father and son rebels were stirring the people. The powers-that-be were getting nervous.

"Young black men are dying because they refuse to take the lash anymore," Omoro preached the unwittingly personal prophecy from Compton to Oakland. "Snatch that lash out of the air! Stand up and stare into eyes hidden behind evil and guile."

And so Sadikifu Omoro, new president of UCLA's Black Student Union, inspired by the words of his father, refused to take the lash anymore, snatched it out of the air, stood up, and stared into eyes hidden behind evil and guile.

"Stand up to injustice! Fight back to the death!" Omoro preached to the converted, including his son.

But when campus police called him on what he preached, Omoro had to face what he really was made of.

Sadikifu died—beaten to death by campus police, beaten beyond anything his father knew, beaten like young black men are in the land that enslaved them.

Suddenly Lamont Lester-Allegro realized, even as the party buzzed around him—around them—the truth that Raymond Harris Sr. represented. He could see the clear truth reflected in the ex-Panther's honey-colored eyes, eyes that sparkled with pain, loss, and loneliness permeated by guilt. It was a self-hate of its own. It was a self-hate Lamont once knew so well, a self-hate not to be forgotten but learned from so that if it ever reared its ugly head again, it can be fought against by a warrior who knew its strategies.

The eyes of Raymond Harris Sr. begged to cry but somehow didn't know how, could not yet bear to. Still, after all these years. Oh how well Lamont understood this too. And how he now ached for this man, yet felt good for him. Who better knew the meaning of darkest before the dawn?

And suddenly Lamont could see so clearly the son. He could see the junior. He could see the mother. He could see his own wife. Although he did not fully understand what he saw, he did fully understand and was grateful for the deep caring he had for them all, inexplicitly yet unconditionally.

Something inside Lamont made him bring his hand up gently to Raymond's lips, in a gentle, halting little gesture. Raymond was brought to grateful doe-eye attention by the move.

Lamont then shed a single empathetic tear, and from this a new strength appeared. A strength Lamont had not quite known before, nor could have even imagined. It was a strength that made him think beyond himself. Raymond was his brother and he, the keeper. And so he took his brother in his arms and then, and only then, was Raymond allowed to shed the tears he had not allowed himself to shed: tears for his son, tears for himself for condemning his soul to take the blame for what was blameless. What Sadikifu had believed he believed from the bottom of his heart. And it was a noble belief. That the son learned to believe as the father believed was no crime. That the son died for the beliefs he had learned from the father was an honorable thing. Raymond Harris Sr. knew that now. His tears told him so.

And then suddenly Lamont knew what it was. He knew what he felt when his wife would come visit him at night in his dreams and his nightmares. He knew what it was that she brought. He knew what it was that he felt just as sure as the Santa Ana winds blow when they want to. He knew. He felt . . . her forgiveness.

For the first time in his life Lamont felt free to experience unconditional love, given and received. The comfort and support he and Raymond provided each other defied society's oppression and they lived their lives as openly gay men in a committed relationship built on deep caring, buoyed by personal strengths ever burgeoning, blessed by a perfect God unsubjected to imperfect man's condemnations. And there was the added gift of a sweet lovemaking neither partner had experienced before.

The good black people of Baldwin Hills got over it. Had to. Times had changed, were changing, and the corpses of intolerance lined along the side of the road known as the future, were picked at by unprejudiced vultures, bones left to brittle and break and dissolve into the dust of the ground.

Those yesterday Negroes and trailer-trash yahoos who managed to breathe for so long now breathed a death-rattle foulness. Kicking and screaming, their one foot in the grave of their own misery-making felt the sting of the hellfire they'd kindled.

When San Francisco's mayor defied President Bush's edict masked as urging, Lamont and Raymond were one of the state's first same-sex couples to marry. Their civil ceremony was flashed throughout the nation and they were known as that handsome black couple from Baldwin Hills. The black bourgeois enclave was forced out of the closet of perceived conservatism, yet no one in the community was worsened by it, except maybe Abner Lester-Allegro. His cold-blooded heart attacked him with a vengeance when he saw Lamont and Raymond seal it with a kiss on the five o'clock news. The attendant stroke rendered him to mumblings from a wheelchair and round-the-clock services of uncaring caretakers.

Lamont looked in on his father daily. The hatred he thought he had for him, Lamont had long since realized, was a hatred he had had for himself, a hatred that no longer existed, replaced by self-love and the love of his man.

Forgiveness was beginning to spread all around.

The company's main offices faced the County Art Museum on Wilshire Boulevard. The staff, a sea of multicolored buppies, buzzed about with the cool and calm of Stepfords. The company had long been structured to operate on automatic, fueled by these well-paid worker bees whose queen was pure benevolence.

The elder Lester-Allegro, Doctor Abner, though recovered somewhat from the stroke, was still too infirm for much of anything. Too infirm to come to board meetings, hold public office, or to painlessly piss. Too infirm to remember the pains he had caused. Too infirm to know he too had been forgiven. So Lamont would make the appearance at the office, having assumed the position of president of the Lester-Allegro

Group. He would smile and greet and show genuine concern for the smallest situation with the most unseniored employee. And it was a true interest. He had come too far to give up the smell of the roses, the brush of the sea breeze, the tale of a child crying and playing and sleeping and laughing. He had come too far up the mountain. And he knew that he was better for the journey, and respectful and regretful of the lives he had beached. He knew that whatever he would be called upon to do, whatever recompense was due, whatever the penitence, he was ready to deliver from the deepest resources of his heart and soul. He had gotten past the bitter and had reached the sweet.

So he stood on the rock and looked toward the sun. The clean breeze of the high air swirled gently around him, whispering to him like angels pointing him toward grace. He then looked down at the world minuscule below. It was a beautiful lush of rolling hills, swimming pools, palm trees, and ocean. He was not afraid anymore, not afraid of living. And the realization made him shake, vibrated him. Something wonderful was brewing deep inside him and causing his veins to tingle with a wanting.

And then they came. In great buckets came tears. He shook and cried and wailed like a feel-too-good Baptist preacher at Christmas morning service.

As the sun smiled down on him he smiled right back up, and the tears ran past his smile, down his neck, over his bosom. He then stretched out his arms and received all that the sun was giving. And for the first time, for the very first time . . . he was truly living life with his eyes and heart wide open. He had love on his side.

He had wings.

Epilogue

I t is often said Los Angeles has no ghettos, and this is nearly true. You would be hard pressed to find alleys in Los Angeles County, save for, ironically, Beverly Hills. Tenements, such as they are, are stucco haciendas surrounded by flower gardens and palm trees. The homeless of the city do not starve or freeze. They can always pick fruit off trees that grow abundantly in city parks in a year-round eighty-degree climate.

It is also often said that it never rains in Southern California. Well, this is simply not the case. It *rarely* rains in Southern California. It only rains enough to tease the thirsty, like Dorian's dick pulled away from the flickering tip of Ricardo Mathis' outstretched tongue.

What is said about black Los Angeles and what is true about black Los Angeles have always made for lively debate, a debate kept alive by Ricardo Mathis. He finally wrote the novel years of writing brilliant short stories and essays had prepared him for.

He never identified Baldwin Hills as Baldwin Hills in his

first long-form work, not that Baldwin Hills of this day really cared. It was so much better to fictionalize the little he knew and maintain a hush-hush expertise that could not be challenged.

Like everyone else, Ricardo felt the loss of Dorian Moore. He was compelled by fond memories and projected wealth to write about it and the effect this loss had on L.A.'s proper blacks. The sex was just that good, the tale too intriguing.

The immortalization of Dorian Moore, renamed Delroy Potter, did indeed make Ricardo Mathis rich. His torrid first novel, *In Search of Pretty Young Black Men*, was an instant bestseller. It told a fascinating story that was less roman à clef than erotic fantasy. Outside of the late Dorian Moore and the unexplained man watching them fucking that inspiring night, Ricardo knew or had seen none of the key players in this dramedy of manners and morals.

In Ricardo's book, and to this day, the death of Dorian Moore remains a uniquely Los Angeles mystery, like the Black Dahlia case. And those three—Maggie, Lamont, and Elaine—were not the only ones to believe that they had separately killed him. The ending—or endings—to the real story of Dorian Moore are *Rashomon*-esque.

Perhaps one's belief in committing this crime, one's secret confession that "I killed the boy," could be the only and truest way to eat from the boy, digest a piece of him so as to be nourished by him when the world offered precious little nourishment for the boy-hungry multitudes.

Was he a god, or was he just another piece of trade? Maybe Dorian Moore was one and the same; after all, gods and trade both provide comfort.

Whatever he was, he was much-needed pleasure for all. The women loved him and the men loved him. He had something for everyone. And everyone had something for him: teeth, anger, appetite, jealousy, fantasy, fear, hunger, gratitude.

The cannibalizing of Dorian Moore, and morsels like him, will continue. It is the law of nature that these are grown for the nourishment of others.

Thankfully, these morsels are self-replenishing. And they will continue to sprout, if greed is checked often, gluttony arrested, and the too desperate held at arm's length. For to reduce the flow of pretty young black men, to hasten their extinction through the inevitable law of diminishing returns, would piss people off. Because without a god to feed on, there are no people. There is no life. Only mirage.